D1718046

THE COMPLETE TIMON OF ATHENS

An Annotated Edition of the Shakespeare Play

DONALD J. RICHARDSON

authorHOUSE®

AuthorHouse™
1663 Liberty Drive
Bloomington, IN 47403
www.authorhouse.com
Phone: 1 (800) 839-8640

Published by AuthorHouse 03/06/2017

ISBN: 978-1-5246-7169-3 (sc)
ISBN: 978-1-5246-7170-9 (hc)
ISBN: 978-1-5246-7168-6 (e)

Library of Congress Control Number: 2017902254

Print information available on the last page.

This book is printed on acid-free paper.

Other Books by Donald J. Richardson

Dust in the Wind, 2001
Rails to Light, 2005
Song of Fools, 2006
Words of Truth, 2007
The Meditation of My Heart, 2008
The Days of Darkness, 2009
The Dying of the Light, 2010
Between the Darkness and the Light, 2011
The Days of Thy Youth, 2012
Those Who Sit in Darkness, 2013
Just a Song at Twilight, 2014
Covered with Darkness, 2015
Behold the Sun, 2016
Approaching Alzheimer's, 2017
The Complete Hamlet, (Revised) 2017
The Complete Macbeth, 2013
The Complete Romeo and Juliet, 2013
The Complete King Lear, 2013
The Complete Julius Caesar, 2013
The Complete Merchant of Venice, 2013
The Complete Midsummer Night's Dream, 2013
The Complete Much Ado About Nothing, 2013
The Complete Twelfth Night, 2014
The Complete Taming of the Shrew, 2014
The Complete Tempest, 2014
The Complete Othello, 2014
The Complete Henry IV, Part One, 2014
The Complete Antony and Cleopatra, 2014
The Complete Comedy of Errors, 2014
The Complete Henry IV, Part Two, 2014
The Complete Henry V, 2014
The Tragedy of Richard the Third, 2015
The Complete Two Gentlemen of Verona, 2015
The Complete Richard the Second, 2015
The Complete Coriolanus, 2015
The Complete As You Like It, 2015

The Complete All's Well That Ends Well, 2015
The Complete Love's Labors Lost, 2015
The Complete Measure for Measure, 2015
The Complete Winter's Tale, 2015
The Complete Henry VIII, 2016
The Complete Troilus and Cressida, 2016
The Complete King John, 2016
The Complete Cymbaline, 2016
The Complete Titus Andronicus, 2016
The Complete Pericles, Prince of Tyre, 2016

Table of Contents

Timon of Athens

ACT I...3

ACT II 62

ACT III 91

ACT IV...142

ACT V 205

Works Cited..239

For everyone reading *Hamlet* for the first time

About the Book

Timon of Athens might be regarded as the ancestor of Moliere's *Les Misanthrope* in that Alceste seems to embody all of the negativity of Timon. Timon also illustrates the error of equating friendship with finances; "He finds that his idealization of friendship has been an illusion" (Mowat, xiv). He is, thus, a man "nobly but unwisely generous" (Hinman, 17). The play, itself, is one "which its author never quite finished" (Hinman, 27).

About the Author

Although he has long been eligible to retire, Donald J. Richardson continues to (try to) teach English Composition at Phoenix College in Arizona. He defines his life through his teaching, his singing, his volunteering, and his grandchildren.

Timon of Athens

ACT I

SCENE I. Athens. A hall in Timon's house.

Enter Poet, Painter, Jeweller, Merchant, and others, at several doors **Several**: "separate" (Bevington, unpaginated)

POET

1 Good day, sir.

PAINTER

2 I am glad you're well.

POET

3 I have not seen you long: how goes the world?

Long: "for a long time" (Riverside, 1,493); **how ... world**: "proverbial for 'How are you?'" (Mowat, 6)

PAINTER

4 It wears, sir, as it grows.

Wears: "wears away, wears out"; **grows**: "grows older" (Riverside, 1,493)

POET

5 Ay, that's well known:

6 But what particular rarity? what strange,

Rarity: "unusual occurrence" (Bevington); **strange**: "i.e., event not experienced before" (Mowat, 6)

7 Which manifold record not matches? See,

Which . . . matches: "i.e. for which the records, though full, offer no precedent" (Riverside, 1,493)

8 Magic of bounty! all these spirits thy power

Bounty: "generosity (Timon's)" (Riverside, 1,493); **spirits**: "i.e., beings, persons (spoken of as if they were spiritis conjured by magic)" (Bevington); **thy power**: "i.e., the power of the bounty dispensed by Timon" (Wright, 1)

9 Hath conjur'd to attend. I know the merchant.

Conjur'd: "summoned by a simple spell" (Riverside, 1,493)

PAINTER

10 I know them both; th' other's a jeweller.

MERCHANT

11 O, 'tis a worthy lord.

Worthy lord: "i.e., Timon" (Bevington)

JEWELLER

12 Nay, that's most fix'd.

Fix'd: "certain" (Riverside, 1,493)

MERCHANT

13 A most incomparable man, breath'd, as it were,

Breath'd: "trained by exercise" (Riverside, 1,493); "animated, inspired" (Mowat, 6)

14 To an untirable and continuate goodness:

Untirable: "tireless" (Mowat, 6); **continuate**: "continuous, habitual"; **goodness**: "bounty" (Riverside, 1,493)

15 He passes.

Passes: "excels"
(Riverside, 1,493);
"surpasses (anyone)"
(Wright, 1)

JEWELLER

16 I have a jewel here--

MERCHANT

17 O, pray, let's see't: for the Lord Timon, sir?

JEWELLER

18 If he will touch the estimate: but, for that--

Touch the estimate:
"meet the price"
(Riverside, 1,493)

POET

19 [Reciting to himself] "When we for recompense
have

When . . . good: "i.e.,
false praise in real life
lowers the value of
poetry that praises truly"
(Hinman, 32)

20 prais'd the vild,

Vild: "vile" (Riverside,
1,493)

21 It stains the glory in that happy verse

Happy: "(more)
appropriate to its
occasion" (Riverside,
1,493)

22 Which aptly sings the good."

Aptly: "fitly, i.e.
truthfully" (Riverside,
1,493); **sings**: "i.e., **sings**
of" (Mowat, 8); "praises"
(Wright, 2)

MERCHANT

23 'Tis a good form.

Form: "kind; shape;
quality" (Mowat, 8)

Looking at the jewel

5

JEWELLER

24 And rich: here is a water, look ye.

Water: "transparent luster (such as characterizes a diamond)" (Wright, 2)

PAINTER

25 You are rapt, sir, in some work, some dedication

Rapt: "engrossed" (Riverside, 1,493); **dedication**: "i.e., **dedication** of a poem (**work**) to a patron" (Mowat, 8)

26 To the great lord.

POET

27 A thing slipp'd idly from me.

Idly: "casually" (Bevington)

28 Our poesy is as a gum, which oozes

Gum . . . nourish'd: "This figure of speech perhaps refers to the sap secreted by trees and shrubs." (Mowat, 8); **oozes**: "issues naturally and effortlessly" (Wright, 2)

29 From whence 'tis nourish'd: the fire i' the flint

30 Shows not till it be struck; our gentle flame

It: "i.e., the **flint**" (Mowat, 8); **gentle**: "noble" (Riverside, 1,493)

31 Provokes itself and like the current flies

Provokes itself: "i.e. needs no external stimulus, as the flint does"; **flies**: "seeks to escape from" (Riverside, 1,493)

32 Each bound it chases. What have you there?

Bound: "bank"; **chases**: "i.e. seems to direct itself toward. Many editors adopt Theobald's emendation *chafes*, 'frets against.'" (Riverside, 1,493)

PAINTER

33 A picture, sir. When comes your book forth?

POET

34 Upon the heels of my presentment, sir.

Upon . . . presentment: "as soon as I have presented the poem (to Timon)" (Riverside, 1,494)

35 Let's see your piece.

PAINTER

36 'Tis a good piece.

POET

37 So 'tis: this comes off well and excellent.

Comes off: "turns out" (Williams, 2); **and excellent**: "excellently well" (Hinman, 32)

PAINTER

38 Indifferent.

Indifferent: "not bad" (Riverside, 1,494)

POET

39 Admirable: how this grace

This grace: "i.e., of the person in the picture" (Bevington)

40 Speaks his own standing! what a mental power

Speaks . . . standing: "expressed the dignity of the sitter (probably Timon)" (Riverside, 1,494); **standing**: "position" (Williams, 2)

41 This eye shoots forth! how big imagination

Big: "i.e., forcefully" (Mowat, 8); **imagination / Moves in this lip**: "this lip expresses what the subject is thinking" (Wright, 2)

42 Moves in this lip! to the dumbness of the gesture

Moves in: "is suggested by" (Hinman, 33); **to . . . interpret**: "i.e. the gesture, though silent, is so expressive that one could easily supply words to fit" (Riverside,1,494)

43 One might interpret.

Interpret: "supply words" (Charney, 43)

PAINTER

44 It is a pretty mocking of the life.

Mocking: "imitation" (Riverside, 1,494)

45 Here is a touch; is't good?

Touch: "detail, stroke or dash of color" (Mowat, 8)

POET

46 I will say of it,

47 It tutors nature: artificial strife

Artificial strife: "the striving of art (to outdo nature)" (Riverside, 1,494)

48 Lives in these touches, livelier than life

Lives: "achieves the level of life, equals nature"; **livelier than life**: "more lifelike than life itself" (Riverside, 1,494).

Enter certain Senators, and pass over

PAINTER

49 How this lord is follow'd!

Follow'd: "i.e., sought after by admirers" (Mowat, 10)

POET

50 The senators of Athens: happy men!

Happy men: "i.e. the senators are fortunate in being friends of Timon. Many editors accept Theobald's emendation of *men* to *man*—Timon is fortunate in having senators among his 'followers.'" (Riverside, 1,494)

PAINTER

51 Look, moe!

Moe: "more" (Riverside, 1,494); "others" (Wright, 3)

POET

52 You see this confluence, this great flood

53 of visitors.

54 I have, in this rough work, shaped out a man,

Shaped out: "formed" (Mowat, 10)

55 Whom this beneath world doth embrace and hug

Beneath world: "Cf. 'under globe' in *King Lear*, II.ii.163. In the Ptolemaic astronomy the earth was seen as under the moon's sphere, and the sublunary region was the only part of the universe subject to change." (Riverside, 1,494)

56 With amplest entertainment: my free drift

Entertainment: "hospitality; support" (Mowat, 10); **drift**: "flow of meaning" (Riverside, 1,494); **my free ... behind**: "i.e., I attack no single individual but rise far above the particular" (Mowat, 10)

57 Halts not particularly, but moves itself

Particularly: "at particular persons"; **moves ... wax**: "i.e. ranges widely, as in writing not limited by the small size of the wax tablet used (?). A much disputed passage." (Riverside, 1,494)

58 In a wide sea of wax: no levell'd malice

Levell'd: "aimed (at a single person)" (Riverside, 1,494)

59 Infects one comma in the course I hold;

Comma: "detail" (Riverside, 1,494); **hold**: "pursue" (Wright, 3)

60 But flies an eagle flight, bold and forth on,

Flies: "it flies, i.e. my course is" (Riverside, 1,494); **forth on**: "directly on, without interruption" (Mowat, 10)

61 Leaving no tract behind.

Tract: "trace, track" (Riverside, 1,494)

PAINTER

62 How shall I understand you?

How ... you: "what do you mean" (Bevington)

POET

63 I will unbolt to you.

Unbolt: "unlock, lay open" (Riverside, 1,494); "explain" (Hinman, 33)

64 You see how all conditions, how all minds,

Conditions: "temperaments, characters" (Riverside, 1,494); "social levels" (Hinman, 33)

65 As well of glib and slippery creatures as

66 Of grave and austere quality, tender down

Quality: "disposition" (Mowat, 10); **tender down**: "offer" (Riverside, 1,494)

67 Their services to Lord Timon: his large fortune

68 Upon his good and gracious nature hanging

Hanging: "The poem speaks as though Timon's wealth were a mere appendage to his virtues, but the reader is meant to see that in truth Timon's fortune 'hangs upon' him like a cloak and is more conspicuous to his beholders than is his inner worth." (Wright, 3)

69 Subdues and properties to his love and tendance

Properties ... tendance: "makes his own to love him and attend on him" (Riverside, 1,494); **properties**: "appropriates"; **tendance**: "attention, care" (Mowat, 10)

70 All sorts of hearts; yea, from the glass-fac'd flatterer

Glass-fac'd: "mirror-faced (because he reflects the desires and moods of the flattered)" (Riverside, 1,494)

71 To Apemantus, that few things loves better

72 Than to abhor himself: even he drops down

Abhor himself: "give himself occasion to feel disgust (which, of course, Timon's smug acceptance of flattery does inspire in Apemantus)." (Wright, 3)

73 The knee before him, and returns in peace

Returns: "departs" (Riverside, 1,494)

74 Most rich in Timon's nod.

In Timon's nod: "for having been acknowledged by Timon" (Bevington)

PAINTER

75 I saw them speak together.

POET

76 Sir, I have upon a high and pleasant hill

77 Feign'd Fortune to be throned: the base o' the mount

Feign'd: "imagined" (Charney, 44); "represented in fiction"; **Fortune**: "the goddess Fortuna, who whimsically awards success or failure to individuals" (Mowat, 12)

78 Is rank'd with all deserts, all kind of natures,

Rank'd . . . deserts: "lined with men of all degrees of merit" (Riverside, 1,494)

79 That labor on the bosom of this sphere

This sphere: "i.e., the earth" (Bevington)

80 To propagate their states: amongst them all,

Propagate: "multiply"; **states**: "fortunes" (Riverside, 1,494)

81 Whose eyes are on this sovereign lady fix'd,

82 One do I personate of Lord Timon's frame,

Personate: "represent"; **frame**: "mental and physical nature" (Riverside, 1,494)

83 Whom Fortune with her ivory hand wafts to her;

Ivory hand: "the ivory (white) hand signifies favor; presumably, the other hand is black and distributes ill luck. Fortune was often depicted with two faces, or a bisected face, and sometimes many-handed, to symbolize the uncertainty of her favor" (Wright, 4); **wafts**: "waves, beckons" (Riverside, 1,494)

84 Whose present grace to present slaves and servants

Whose: "i.e. Fortune's"; **grace**: "favor (to the man representing Timon)"; **to . . . rivals**: "transforms his rivals instantly into slaves and servants" (Riverside, 1,494); **present**: "immediate" (Wright, 4)

85 Translates his rivals.

Translates: "transforms" (Wright, 4)

PAINTER

86 'Tis conceived to scope.

To scope: "fittingly" (Riverside, 1,494)

87 This throne, this Fortune, and this hill, methinks,

Methinks: "i.e., it seems to me" (Mowat, 12)

88 With one man beckon'd from the rest below,

89 Bowing his head against the steepy mount

Bowing his head: "i.e., straining"; **steepy**: "steep" (Mowat, 12)

13

90 To climb his happiness, would be well express'd

Climb his happiness: "attain his good fortune by climbing" (Wright, 4); **would . . . condition**: "would be closely paralleled by our situation in the real world" (Hinman, 34)

91 In our condition.

Our condition: "i.e. the human condition (but some take it to mean the painter's profession)" (Riverside, 1,494)

POET

92 Nay, sir, but hear me on.

On: "further" (Mowat, 12)

93 All those which were his fellows but of late,

Which: "i.e., who"; **fellows**: "equals"; **but of late**: "only lately" (Mowat, 12)

94 Some better than his value, on the moment

Better . . . value: "worth more than he" (Riverside, 1,494); **on the moment**: "straightaway" (Mowat, 12)

95 Follow his strides, his lobbies fill with tendance,

His . . . tendance: "i.e. crowd into his house to offer their services" (Riverside, 1,494); **tendance**: "attendants" (Mowat, 12)

96 Rain sacrificial whisperings in his ear,

Rain . . . ear: "shower him with murmurs of adoration, as though he were a god" (Wright, 4)

97 Make sacred even his stirrup, and through him

Make . . . stirrup: "i.e. perform with reverence even the menial duty of helping him to mount his horse"; **through . . . air**: "act as if it were by his courtesy that they breathed the air (which we know to be free)" (Riverside, 1,494)

98 Drink the free air.

Drink: "breathe" (Charney, 45)

PAINTER

99 Ay, marry, what of these?

Marry: "indeed (originally the name of the Virgin Mary used as an oath)" (Riverside, 1,494)

POET

100 When Fortune in her shift and change of mood

101 Spurns down her late beloved, all his dependants

Spurns down: "tramples, kicks" (Mowat, 12)

102 Which labor'd after him to the mountain's top

103 Even on their knees and hands, let him slip down,

104 Not one accompanying his declining foot.

Declining: "descending, falling" (Mowat, 12)

PAINTER

105 'Tis common:

106 A thousand moral paintings I can show

Moral: "allegorical" (Riverside, 1,494)

107 That shall demonstrate these quick blows of Fortune's

Quick: "(1) swift (2) full of life" (Charney, 45)

108 More pregnantly than words. Yet you do well

Pregnantly: "significantly" (Wright, 5); "cogently" (Hinman, 35)

15

109 To show Lord Timon that mean eyes have seen	**Mean**: "lowly" (Riverside, 1,494)
110 The foot above the head.	**The foot . . . head**: "i.e. the great man falling headlong" (Riverside, 1,494)

Trumpets sound. Enter TIMON, addressing himself courteously to every suitor; a Messenger from VENTIDIUS talking with him; LUCILIUS and other servants following

TIMON

111 Imprison'd is he, say you?

MESSENGER

112 Ay, my good lord: five talents is his debt,	**Talents**: "A talent might be taken, very roughly, as $2000 in modern money." (Riverside, 1,495)
113 His means most short, his creditors most strait:	**Short**: "limited" (Bevington); **strait**: "unyielding, insistent" (Riverside, 1,495); "strict" (Charney, 46)
114 Your honorable letter he desires	**Your . . . letter**: "i.e., a **letter** from **your** Honor (i.e., you)" (Mowat, 14)
115 To those have shut him up; which failing,	**Those**: "those who" (Riverside, 1,495); **which failing**: "i.e., the lack of which" (Mowat, 14)
116 Periods his comfort.	**Periods**: "puts an end to" (Riverside, 1,495)

TIMON

117 Noble Ventidius! Well;

118 I am not of that feather to shake off	**Feather**: "type, disposition" (Riverside, 1,495); "character" (Charney, 46)

119 My friend when he must need me. I do know him   **Know him**: "i.e., **know him** to be" (Mowat, 14)

120 A gentleman that well deserves a help:

121 Which he shall have: I'll pay the debt,

122 and free him.

MESSENGER

123 Your lordship ever binds him.   **Binds**: "ties him to gratitude (by freeing him)" (Riverside, 1,495)

TIMON

124 Commend me to him: I will send his ransom;   **Commend me**: "express my regards" (Riverside, 1,495)

125 And being enfranchised, bid him come to me.   **Enfranchised**: "set free" (Bevington)

126 'Tis not enough to help the feeble up,

127 But to support him after. Fare you well.   **But**: "i.e. but it is necessary also" (Riverside, 1,495)

MESSENGER

128 All happiness to your honor!

Exit

Enter an old Athenian

OLD ATHENIAN

129 Lord Timon, hear me speak.

TIMON

130 Freely, good father.   **Freely**: "readily, glady" (Bevington); **father**: "respectful term of address to an old man" (Mowat, 14)

OLD ATHENIAN

131 Thou hast a servant named Lucilius.

17

TIMON

132 I have so: what of him?

OLD ATHENIAN

133 Most noble Timon, call the man before thee.

TIMON

134 Attends he here, or no? Lucilius!

LUCILIUS

135 Here, at your lordship's service.

OLD ATHENIAN

136 This fellow here, Lord Timon, this thy creature,

Creature: "dependent (contemptuous)" (Riverside, 1,495)

137 By night frequents my house. I am a man

138 That from my first have been inclined to thrift;

From my first: "i.e., **from** the beginning of **my** life" (Mowat, 16)

139 And my estate deserves an heir more rais'd

More rais'd: "of higher social status" (Riverside, 1,495)

140 Than one which holds a trencher.

Holds a trencher: "i.e. waits at table (*trencher* = wooden dish" (Riverside, 1,495)

TIMON

141 Well; what further?

OLD ATHENIAN

142 One only daughter have I, no kin else,

143 On whom I may confer what I have got:

Got: "acquired, amassed" (Mowat, 16)

144 The maid is fair, a' th' youngest for a bride,

Maid: "young woman"; **a' th' . . . bride**: "i.e., only just the age to be marriageable" (Mowat, 16)

145 And I have bred her at my dearest cost

Bred . . . cost: "brought her up and educated her at great expense" (Bevington)

146 In qualities of the best. This man of thine

Qualities: "accomplishments" (Riverside, 1,495)

147 Attempts her love: I prithee, noble lord,

Attempts: "endeavors to obtain or attract" (Mowat, 16)

148 Join with me to forbid him her resort;

Her resort: "access to her" (Mowat, 16)

149 Myself have spoke in vain.

TIMON

150 The man is honest.

Honest: "honorable" (Riverside, 1,495)

OLD ATHENIAN

151 Therefore he will be, Timon:

Therefore . . . be: "i.e. that being so, he will do the honorable thing in this case (and leave my daughter alone)" (Riverside, 1,495)

152 His honesty rewards him in itself;

His honesty . . . itself: "Proverbial: 'Virtue is its own reward.'" (Mowat, 16)

153 It must not bear my daughter.

Bear my daughter: "i.e., carry off **my daughter** as well" (Mowat, 16)

TIMON

154 Does she love him?

OLD ATHENIAN

155 She is young and apt:

Apt: "impressionable" (Riverside, 1,495)

156 Our own precedent passions do instruct us

Precedent: "experienced in the past" (Riverside, 1,495); "former" (Bevington)

157 What levity's in youth.

Levity: "instability" (Wright, 7)

TIMON

158 [To LUCILIUS] Love you the maid?

LUCILIUS

159 Ay, my good lord, and she accepts of it.

Accepts of it: "receives it favorably" (Mowat, 16)

OLD ATHENIAN

160 If in her marriage my consent be missing,

161 I call the gods to witness, I will choose

162 Mine heir from forth the beggars of the world,

163 And dispossess her all.

All: "entirely" (Riverside, 1,495)

TIMON

164 How shall she be endowed,

How . . . endowed: "what dowry shall she have" (Riverside, 1,495)

165 if she be mated with an equal husband?

Equal husband: "i.e., **husband** of her own status" (Mowat, 16)

OLD ATHENIAN

166 Three talents on the present; in future, all.

Three talents: "(about $6,000)" (Hinman, 37); **on the present**: "immediately" (Riverside, 1,495)

TIMON

167 This gentleman of mine hath served me long:

168 To build his fortune I will strain a little,

169 For 'tis a bond in men. Give him thy daughter:

Bond in: "duty of friendship among" (Riverside, 1,495)

170 What you bestow, in him I'll counterpoise,

In him I'll counterpoise: "I'll balance on his behalf." (Wright, 7)

171 And make him weigh with her.

Weigh with her: "i.e., equal her (dowry's) weight in the scales (The image is of a balance with scales, on which the daughter's dowry is counterpoised by Timon's gift." (Mowat, 18)

OLD ATHENIAN

172 Most noble lord,

173 Pawn me to this your honor, she is his.

Pawn . . . honor: "if you will give me your word of honor to do this" (Riverside, 1,495)

TIMON

174 My hand to thee; mine honor on my promise.

LUCILIUS

175 Humbly I thank your lordship: never may

176 That state or fortune fall into my keeping,

That: "i.e., any" (Bevington); **state**: "prosperous condition" (Mowat, 18)

177 Which is not owed to you!

Owed to you: "(1) acknowledged as issuing from your generosity; (2) due to you as a debt" (Riverside, 1,495)

Exeunt LUCILIUS and Old Athenian

POET

178 Vouchsafe my labor, and long live your lordship!

> **Vouchsafe**: "deign to accept" (Riverside, 1,495)

TIMON

179 I thank you; you shall hear from me anon:

> **Anon**: "soon" (Mowat, 18)

180 Go not away. What have you there, my friend?

PAINTER

181 A piece of painting, which I do beseech

> **Piece of painting**: "i.e., **painting** (literally, example of **painting**)" (Mowat, 18)

182 Your lordship to accept.

TIMON

183 Painting is welcome.

184 The painting is almost the natural man;

> **Natural man**: "**man** free of affectation or artificiality" (Mowat, 18)

185 or since dishonor traffics with man's nature,

> **Dishonor . . . nature**: "i.e., men are corrupted by dishonorable dealings" (Wright, 8); **traffics**: "deals (improperly)" (Bevington)

186 He is but outside: these pencill'd figures are

> **But outside**: "only what he lets appear"; **pencill'd**: "painted" (Riverside, 1,495)

187 Even such as they give out. I like your work;

> **Give out**: "i.e., profess (to be)" (Mowat, 18)

188 And you shall find I like it: wait attendance

> **Wait attendance**: "i.e., **wait** (a phrase addressed to an inferior)" (Mowat, 18)

189 Till you hear further from me.

PAINTER

190 The gods preserve ye!

TIMON

191 Well fare you, gentleman: give me your hand;

192 We must needs dine together. Sir, your jewel — **Must needs**: "i.e., **must**" (Mowat, 20)

193 Hath suffered under praise. — **Suffered under**: "i.e. been overwhelmed by. (The Jeweller misunderstands.)" (Riverside, 1,495)

JEWELLER

194 What, my lord! dispraise?

TIMON

195 A mere saciety of commendations. — **Mere saciety**: "utter satiety" (Riverside, 1,495)

196 If I should pay you for't as 'tis extoll'd,

197 It would unclew me quite. — **Unclew**: "ruin (literally, unwind)" (Mowat, 20)

JEWELLER

198 My lord, 'tis rated

199 As those which sell would give: but you well know, — **As ... give**: "at the price the seller would be ready to pay for it" (Riverside, 1,495)

200 Things of like value differing in the owners — **Like**: "the same" (Mowat, 20)

201 Are prized by their masters: believe't, dear lord, — **Prized ... masters**: "valued according to the status of their wearers" (Riverside, 1,495)

23

202 You mend the jewel by the wearing it.

Mend: "increase the value of" (Riverside, 1,495)

TIMON

203 Well mock'd.

Well mock'd: "an excellent performance" (Riverside, 1,495)

MERCHANT

204 No, my good lord; he speaks the common tongue,

The common tongue: "what everybody says" (Riverside, 1,496)

205 Which all men speak with him.

TIMON

206 Look, who comes here: will you be chid?

Chid: "chided, scolded" (Mowat, 20)

Enter APEMANTUS

JEWELLER

207 We'll bear, with your lordship.

Bear with: "suffer along with" (Riverside, 1,496); "i.e., endure" (Mowat, 20)

MERCHANT

208 He'll spare none.

TIMON

209 Good morrow to thee, gentle Apemantus!

Morrow: "morning" (Mowat, 20); **gentle**: "courteous" (Wright, 9)

APEMANTUS

210 Till I be gentle, stay thou for thy good morrow;

Stay . . . morrow: "i.e., you can wait for me to say 'good morning'" (Mowat, 20)

211 When thou art Timon's dog, and these knaves honest.

When . . . honest: "i.e., **when** the impossible happens" (Mowat, 20)

TIMON

212 Why dost thou call them knaves? thou know'st them not.

APEMANTUS

213 Are they not Athenians?

TIMON

214 Yes.

APEMANTUS

215 Then I repent not.

Repent not: "don't regret what I said" (Bevington)

216 Jeweller: You know me, Apemantus?

APEMANTUS

217 Thou know'st I do: I call'd thee by thy name.

Thy name: "i.e knave" (Riverside, 1,496)

TIMON

218 Thou art proud, Apemantus.

APEMANTUS

219 Of nothing so much as that I am not like Timon.

TIMON

220 Whither art going?

Art: "i.e., are you" (Mowat, 22)

APEMANTUS

221 To knock out an honest Athenian's brains.

TIMON

222 That's a deed thou't die for.

Thou't: "thou wilt" (Riverside, 1,496)

Donald J. Richardson

APEMANTUS

223 Right, if doing nothing be death by the law.

Nothing: "(1) nothing (since no honest Athenian exists); (2) wickedness" (Wright, 9); **death by the law**: "subject to the death penalty. (Athenians have no brains; therefore to knock out their brains is to do nothing.)" (Bevington)

TIMON

224 How likest thou this picture, Apemantus?

APEMANTUS

225 The best, for the innocence.

Innocence: "harmlessness (in which, he implies, it differs from real life)" (Riverside, 1,496); "artlessness" (Mowat, 22); "stupidity" (Williams, 9)

TIMON

226 Wrought he not well that painted it?

Wrought: "worked" (Mowat, 22)

APEMANTUS

227 He wrought better that made the painter; and yet

228 he's but a filthy piece of work.

Filthy: "contemptible" (Charney, 50)

PAINTER

229 Y'r a dog.

A dog: "Alluding to Apemantus' being a cynic philosopher; *cynic* is derived from the Greek word for 'dog.'" (Riverside, 1,496)

APEMANTUS

230 Thy mother's of my generation: what's she, if I
    be a dog?

Of my generation: "(1)
my coeval; (2) of my
species" (Riverside,
1,496)

TIMON

231 Wilt dine with me, Apemantus?

APEMANTUS

232 No; I eat not lords.

Eat not lords: "i.e. do not
consume their substance"
(Riverside, 1,496)

TIMON

233 And thou shouldst, thou 'ldst anger ladies.

And: "if" (Riverside,
1,496)

APEMANTUS

234 O, they eat lords; so they come by great bellies.

Come by great bellies:
"become pregnant"
(Charney, 51)

TIMON

235 That's a lascivious apprehension.

Apprehension: "(1)
interpretation (2) seizure,
grasp (with a bawdy
suggestion in the idea
of seizing physically)"
(Bevington)

APEMANTUS

236 So thou apprehendest it: take it for thy labor.

TIMON

237 How dost thou like this jewel, Apemantus?

APEMANTUS

238 Not so well as plain-dealing, which will not cast a

Plain-dealing: "alluding to the saying 'Plain dealing is a jewel.'";
cast: "Almost all editors adopt the F3 reading *cost*, but *cast* receives some support from a longer variant of the proverb quoted just above: 'Plain dealing is a jewel, but they that use it die beggars.' Possibly Apemantus plays on both senses to contrast the conventional advantage (it makes one no poorer) with what he sees as the true advantage (it makes one no richer)." (Riverside, 1,496)

239 man a doit.

Doit: "small coin worth a fraction of a penny" (Riverside, 1,496)

TIMON

240 What dost thou think 'tis worth?

APEMANTUS

241 Not worth my thinking. How now, poet!

POET

242 How now, philosopher!

APEMANTUS

243 Thou liest.

POET

244 Art not one?

APEMANTUS

245 Yes.

POET

246 Then I lie not.

APEMANTUS

247 Art not a poet?

POET

248 Yes.

APEMANTUS

249 Then thou liest: look in thy last work, where thou

Then thou liest: "because poets only feign truth" (Riverside, 1,496); "(a play on the old idea that poetry is a *mimesis*, imitation, mocking, or feigning of reality and therefore a lie)" (Charney,52)

250 hast feigned him a worthy fellow.

Him: "i.e., Timon" (Mowat, 22)

POET

251 That's not feigned; he is so.

APEMANTUS

252 Yes, he is worthy of thee, and to pay thee for thy

253 labor: he that loves to be flattered is worthy o'

254 the flatterer. Heavens, that I were a lord!

TIMON

255 What wouldst do then, Apemantus?

APEMANTUS

256 E'en as Apemantus does now; hate a lord with my heart.

TIMON

257 What, thyself?

APEMANTUS

258 Ay.

TIMON

259 Wherefore?

Wherefore: "why" (Mowat, 24)

APEMANTUS

260 That I had no angry wit to be a lord.

No . . . lord: "that in being a lord I forfeited the angry wit (which I have now). Many editors emend *no angry wit*, adopting Theobald's *so hungry a wit* or Deighton's *my angry will*." (Riverside, 1,496)

261 Art not thou a merchant?

MERCHANT

262 Ay, Apemantus.

APEMANTUS

263 Traffic confound thee, if the gods will not!

Traffic: "trade, business"; **confound**: "ruin" (Riverside, 1,496)

MERCHANT

264 If traffic do it, the gods do it.

APEMANTUS

265 Traffic's thy god; and thy god confound thee!

Trumpet sounds. Enter a Messenger

TIMON

266 What trumpet's that?

MESSENGER

267 'Tis Alcibiades, and some twenty horse,

Horse: "horsemen" (Wright, 11)

268 All of companionship.

Of companionship: "in one party" (Riverside, 1,496)

TIMON

269 Pray, entertain them; give them guide to us.

Entertain: "receive, welcome" (Riverside, 1,496); **give them guide**: "conduct **them**" (Mowat, 24)

Exeunt some Attendants

270 You must needs dine with me: go not you hence

271 Till I have thank'd you: when dinner's done,

272 Show me this piece. I am joyful of your sights.

Of your sights: "to see you" (Riverside, 1,496)

Enter ALCIBIADES, with the rest

273 Most welcome, sir!

APEMANTUS

274 So, so, there!

So, so, there: "well, well, look at that (i.e., all the bowing and scraping)" (Bevington)

275 Aches contract and starve your supple joints!

Aches: "pronounced *aitches*"; **starve**: "paralyze, wither" (Riverside, 1,496)

276 That there should be small love 'mongst these

That: "i.e., to think that" (Wright, 11)

277 sweet knaves,

278 And all this courtesy! The strain of man's bred out

Courtesy: "display of politeness"; **bred out**: "degenerated" (Riverside, 1,496); **strain**: "race, stock" (Bevington)

279 Into baboon and monkey.

ALCIBIADES

280 Sir, you have sav'd my longing, and I feed

Sav'd my longing: "brought to fruition my passionate desire" (Riverside, 1,496)

281 Most hungerly on your sight.

Hungerly: "hungrily" (Mowat, 26)

TIMON

282 Right welcome, sir!

283 Ere we depart, we'll share a bounteous time

Depart: "separate" (Mowat, 26)

284 In different pleasures. Pray you, let us in.

Different: "various"; **let us in**: "let us go in" (Riverside, 1,496)

Exeunt all except APEMANTUS

Enter two Lords

FIRST LORD

285 What time o' day is't, Apemantus?

APEMANTUS

286 Time to be honest.

FIRST LORD

287 That time serves still.

That . . . still: "Time always provides **that** opportunity"; **still**: "always" (Mowat, 26)

APEMANTUS

288 The most accursed thou, that still omit'st it.

Most: "i.e., more" (Bevington); **omit'st**: "fail to take advantage of" (Riverside, 1,497)

SECOND LORD

289 Thou art going to Lord Timon's feast?

APEMANTUS

290 Ay, to see meat fill knaves and wine heat fools.

Meat: "food" (Riverside, 1,497)

SECOND LORD

291 Fare thee well, fare thee well.

APEMANTUS

292 Thou art a fool to bid me farewell twice.

SECOND LORD

293 Why, Apemantus?

APEMANTUS

294 Shouldst have kept one to thyself, for I mean to

Shouldst: "i.e., you should" (Mowat, 26)

295 give thee none.

FIRST LORD

296 Hang thyself!

APEMANTUS

297 No, I will do nothing at thy bidding: make thy

298 requests to thy friend.

SECOND LORD

299 Away, unpeaceable dog, or I'll spurn thee hence!

Unpeaceable: "contentious" (Mowat, 26); **spurn**: "kick" (Riverside, 1,497)

APEMANTUS

300 I will fly, like a dog, the heels o' the ass.

Fly: "flee" (Bevington)

Exit

FIRST LORD

301 He's opposite to humanity. Come, shall we in,

Opposite to: "hostile to (?) or the reverse of (?)" (Riverside, 1,497)

302 And taste Lord Timon's bounty? he outgoes

Outgoes: "goes beyond" (Riverside, 1,497)

303 The very heart of kindness.

Heart: "essence" (Bevington)

SECOND LORD

304 He pours it out; Plutus, the god of gold,

Plutus: "Plutus is related . . . to Pluto, the king of the underworld, and represents the wealth of the soil, both mineral and vegetable. . . ." (Asimov, 137)

305 Is but his steward: no meed, but he repays

Meed: "merit, service (?) or gift (?)"; **repays**: "rewards" (Riverside, 1,497)

306 Sevenfold above itself; no gift to him,

307 But breeds the giver a return exceeding

308 All use of quittance.

Use of quittance: "customary rates of repayment. *Use* means both 'usual practice' and 'interest.'" (Riverside, 1,497); **quittance**: "repayment" (Mowat, 28)

FIRST LORD

309 The noblest mind he carries

Carries: "bears within him" (Mowat, 28)

310 That ever govern'd man.

SECOND LORD

311 Long may he live in fortunes! Shall we in?

In fortunes: "fortunate, prosperous (but possibly we should read *In Fortune's*, in the goddess Fortune's mind)" (Hinman, 43)

FIRST LORD

312 I'll keep you company.

Exeunt

SCENE II. A banqueting-room in Timon's house.

Hoboys playing loud music. A great banquet served in; FLAVIUS and others attending; then enter TIMON, ALCIBIADES, Lords, Senators, and VENTIDIUS. Then comes, dropping, after all, APEMANTUS, discontentedly, like himself

Hoboys: "oboes"; *like himself*: "in his ordinary clothes; not attempting to be ceremonious" (Riverside, 1,497); *dropping, after all*: "lingering" (Williams, 13)

VENTIDIUS

1 Most honor'd Timon,

2 It hath pleased the gods to remember my father's age,

3 And call him to long peace.

Long peace: "eternal rest" (Bevington)

4 He is gone happy, and has left me rich:

Gone: "died" (Bevington)

5 Then, as in grateful virtue I am bound

6 To your free heart, I do return those talents,

Free: "generous" (Riverside, 1,497)

7 Doubled with thanks and service, from whose help

Service: "respect, devotion" (Mowat, 28)

8 I derived liberty.

TIMON

9 O, by no means,

10 Honest Ventidius; you mistake my love:

11 I gave it freely ever; and there's none

35

12 Can truly say he gives, if he receives:

Gives . . . receives: "(Cf. Acts 20:35: 'It is more blessed to give than to receive.')" (Bevington)

13 If our betters play at that game, we must not dare

If: "i.e. even if" (Hinman, 44); **our betters**: "those in higher positions of authority, i.e. the senators" (Riverside, 1,497); **that game**: "i.e., receiving back again what they have given" (Mowat, 30)

14 To imitate them; faults that are rich are fair.

Faults . . . fair: "Proverbial: 'Rich men have no **faults**.'" (Mowat, 30); **fair**: "i.e., excused by their wealth" (Bevington)

VENTIDIUS

15 A noble spirit!

TIMON

16 Nay, my lords,

They all stand ceremoniously looking on TIMON

17 Ceremony was but devised at first

Ceremony: "ceremoniousness, formality (This moment in the play is sometimes staged with Timon's guests making elaborately formal gestures of deference to him.)" (Mowat, 30)

18 To set a gloss on faint deeds, hollow welcomes,

Set a gloss on: "give a speciously fair appearance to" (Bevington); **faint**: "half-hearted" (Riverside, 1,497); **hollow**: "insincere" (Wright, 14)

19 Recanting goodness, sorry ere 'tis shown;

Recanting goodness: "generosity that takes back what it has offered" (Bevington)

20 But where there is true friendship, there needs none.

None: "i.e. no ceremony" (Riverside, 1,497)

21 Pray, sit; more welcome are ye to my fortunes

22 Than my fortunes to me.

They sit

FIRST LORD

23 My lord, we always have confess'd it.

Confess'd: "declared. Apemantus quibbles on the word." (Riverside, 1,497)

APEMANTUS

24 Ho, ho, confess'd it! hang'd it, have you not?

Confess'd it! hang'd it: "Proverbial: 'Confess and be hanged.' (In the proverb, *confess* refers to shriving or to admitting to a crime.)" (Mowat, 30)

TIMON

25 O, Apemantus, you are welcome.

APEMANTUS

26 No;

27 You shall not make me welcome:

28 I come to have thee thrust me out of doors.

TIMON

29 Fie, thou'rt a churl; ye've got a humor there

Churl: "surly person" (Bevington); **humor**: "disposition" (Riverside, 1,497)

30 Does not become a man: 'tis much to blame.

Does: "i.e., that **does**"; **much to blame**: "i.e., very blameworthy" (Mowat, 30)

31 They say, my lords, "*ira furor brevis est*;" but yond

Ira . . . est: "Wrath is a brief madness (Horace, *Epistles* 1.2.62)" (Mowat, 30)

32 man is very angry. Go, let him have a table by

Very angry: "i.e. his anger cannot be called a *brief* madness. Many editors follow Rowe in reading *ever angry*." (Riverside, 1,497)

33 himself, for he does neither affect company, nor is

Affect: "(1) like (2) seek, aim at" (Bevington)

34 he fit for't, indeed.

APEMANTUS

35 Let me stay at thine apperil, Timon: I come to

Thine apperil: "your own risk" (Riverside, 1,497)

36 observe; I give thee warning on't.

Observe: "comment" (Wright, 14); **on't**: "i.e., of it" (Mowat, 30)

TIMON

37 I take no heed of thee; thou'rt an Athenian,

38 therefore welcome: I myself would have no power;

Would . . . power: "i.e. do not desire the power to make you silent (which the rule of hospitality forbids)" (Riverside, 1,497)

39 prithee, let my meat make thee silent.

Meat: "food" (Mowat, 30)

APEMANTUS

40 I scorn thy meat; 'twould choke me, for I should

'Twould . . . thee: "i.e., Apemantus would prefer to choke on Timon's meat than to flatter him" (Charney, 56); **for . . . thee**: "i.e. for it is provided for flatterers, and I would be aware that I hadn't paid for it in flattery" (Riverside, 1,497)

41 ne'er flatter thee. O you gods, what a number of

42 men eats Timon, and he sees 'em not! It grieves me

Eats: "i.e., eat" (Mowat, 30)

43 to see so many dip their meat in one man's blood;

One man's blood: "(possible allusion to the Last Supper; the *fellow* in ll. 48-51, who shares food and drink only to betray his host, is like Judas.)" (Bevington)

44 and all the madness is, he cheers them up too.

All the madness: "the height of his madness"; **cheers them up**: "encourages them" (Riverside, 1,497)

45 I wonder men dare trust themselves with men:

46 Methinks they should invite them without knives;

Without knives: "In Shakespeare's day guests brought their own knives." (Riverside, 1,497)

47 Good for their meat, and safer for their lives.

Good: "that would be good" (Williams, 15); **Good . . . meat**: "i.e. the guests would eat less" (Riverside, 1,497); **their meat**: "i.e., the host's food" (Mowat, 32)

Donald J. Richardson

48 There's much example for't; the fellow that sits

49 next him now, parts bread with him, pledges the **Parts**: "shares";
pledges . . . of him:
"i.e., toasts his health"
(Mowat, 32)

50 breath of him in a divided draught, is the readiest **Breath**: "life" (Wright,
15); **divided draught**: "a
drink from a cup that is
passed around the table"
(Charney, 57)

51 man to kill him: 't has been proved. If I were a

52 huge man, I should fear to drink at meals; **Huge**: "great, of high
rank" (Riverside, 1,497)

53 Lest they should spy my windpipe's dangerous **Windpipe's . . . notes**:
notes: "indications on my throat
of where my windpipe
is (and hence where it
might be slit) as the head
is thrown back. (The
windpipe also suggests a
bagpipe capable of notes
of musical sounds.)"
(Bevington)

54 Great men should drink with harness on their **Harness**: "armor"
throats. (Riverside, 1,498)

TIMON

55 My lord, in heart; and let the health go round. **In heart**: "heartily
(spoken as a kind of
toast)" (Riverside, 1,498);
health: "toast, and the
cup" (Bevington)

SECOND LORD

56 Let it flow this way, my good lord. **Let it . . . way**: "may I
be the next to drink your
health" (Wright, 15); **flow**:
"circulate" (Bevington)

40

APEMANTUS

57 Flow this way! A brave fellow! he keeps his tides

Brave: "fine"; **tides**: "times (with a jibe at the Second Lord's use of *flow*)" (Riverside, 1,498); **he keeps . . . / well**: "i.e., he is prompt at offering flattery" (Wright, 15)

58 well. Those healths will make thee and thy state

Those healths . . . ill: "(cf. proverbial 'to drink healths is to drink sickness')" (Hinman, 45); **state**: "condition (including his financial **state**, or his wealth" (Mowat, 32)

59 look ill, Timon. Here's that which is too weak to

Ill: "referring to the proverb 'To drink health is to drink sickness'" (Wright, 15)

60 be a sinner, honest water, which ne'er left man i'
the mire:

Sinner: "causer of sin" (Wright, 15); **i' the mire**: "i.e. in difficulties" (Riverside, 1,498)

61 This and my food are equals; there's no odds:

Odds: "difference, inequality" (Mowat, 32)

62 Feasts are too proud to give thanks to the gods.

Feasts: "i.e. the men who give and attend feasts" (Riverside, 1,497)

Apemantus' grace.

64 Immortal gods, I crave no pelf;

Pelf: "property, possessions" (Bevington)

65 I pray for no man but myself:

66 Grant I may never prove so fond,

Fond: "foolish" (Riverside, 1,498)

67 To trust man on his oath or bond;

68 Or a harlot, for her weeping;

69 Or a dog, that seems a-sleeping:

70 Or a keeper with my freedom;
    Keeper: "jailer" (Riverside, 1,498)

71 Or my friends, if I should need 'em.
    Friends: "proverbial: 'A friend is never known till a man have need.'" (Wright, 16)

72 Amen. So fall to't:
    Fall to't: "i.e., begin to eat" (Bevington)

73 Rich men sin, and I eat root.
    Sin: "i.e., by indulging gluttony" (Wright, 16)

Eats and drinks

74 Much good dich thy good heart, Apemantus!
    Dich: "may it do. (Originally a contraction of 'd' it ye' in the phrase 'much good do it you.')" (Bevington)

TIMON

75 Captain Alcibiades, your heart's in the field now.
    Field: "battlefield" (Mowat, 32)

ALCIBIADES

76 My heart is ever at your service, my lord.

TIMON

77 You had rather be at a breakfast of enemies than a
    Of . . . of: "consisting of . . . with" (Riverside, 1,498)

78 dinner of friends.
    Of friends: "i.e., with friends" (Mowat, 34); **of**: "among" (Bevington)

ALCIBIADES

79 So they were bleeding-new, my lord, there's no
meat

So: "provided" (Riverside, 1,498); **bleeding new**: "freshly killed" (Williams, 16)

80 like 'em: I could wish my best friend at such a feast.

APEMANTUS

81 Would all those flatterers were thine enemies then,

82 that then thou mightst kill 'em and bid me to 'em!

Bid me . . . 'em: "i.e., invite me to eat them" (Mowat, 34)

FIRST LORD

83 Might we but have that happiness, my lord, that you

84 would once use our hearts, whereby we might
express

Use our hearts: "ask some service of our love" (Riverside, 1,498)

85 some part of our zeals, we should think ourselves

Zeals: "devotions" (Wright, 16)

86 for ever perfect.

Perfect: "completely happy" (Riverside, 1,498); "satisfied" (Williams, 16)

TIMON

87 O, no doubt, my good friends, but the gods

88 themselves have provided that I shall have much help

89 from you: how had you been my friends else? Why

How . . . else: "how else could you be accounted my friends" (Wright, 16)

90 have you that charitable title from thousands, did

Charitable: "loving"; **from thousands**: "(only you) out of thousands" (Riverside, 1,498); **from**: "i.e., **from** among" (Mowat, 34)

91 not you chiefly belong to my heart? I have told

Told: "(1) narrated, related; (2) counted" (Mowat, 34)

92 more of you to myself than you can with modesty **Of you**: "i.e., regarding your merits" (Mowat, 34)

93 speak in your own behalf; and thus far I confirm **Confirm / you**: "confirm your claims to be worthy friends" (Riverside, 1,498)

94 you. O you gods, think I, what need we have any **What**: "why" (Riverside, 1,498)

95 friends, if we should ne'er have need of 'em? they

96 were the most needless creatures living, should we **Needless**: "useless" (Bevington)

97 ne'er have use for 'em, and would most resemble

98 sweet instruments hung up in cases that keeps their **Instruments**: "musical instruments"; **keeps**: "i.e., keep" (Mowat, 34)

99 sounds to themselves. Why, I have often wished

100 myself poorer, that I might come nearer to you. **Come nearer to you**: "(1) We create a closer tie with you; (2) know you better, in the sense of detecting their true natures (a sense of which Timon is himself unconscious). Cf. the proverb 'Perfect friendship cannot be without equality.'" (Wright, 17)

101 are born to do benefits: and what better or

102 properer can we call our own than the riches of our **Properer**: "more appropriately" (Mowat, 34)

103 friends? O, what a precious comfort 'tis, to have

104 so many, like brothers, commanding one another's **Commanding**: "having at their disposal" (Bevington)

105 fortunes! O joy, e'en made away ere 't can be born!

Made away: "i.e. dissolved in tears"; **born**: "put into words" (Riverside, 1,498)

106 Mine eyes cannot hold out water, methinks:

Hold out: "resist" (Wright, 17)

107 to forget their faults, I drink to you.

To / forget their faults: "i.e., deliberately to neglect my eyes' weakness" (Mowat, 34) **Faults**: "defects" (Charney, 59)

APEMANTUS

108 Thou weepest to make them drink, Timon.

Thou . . . drink: "i.e. you exude liquid to give them an occasion for absorbing liquid" (Riverside, 1,498)

SECOND LORD

109 Joy had the like conception in our eyes

Had . . . eyes: "had its inception in the same way with tears" (Riverside, 1,498)

110 And at that instant like a babe sprung up.

Sprung up: "(1) leaped in the womb; (2) streamed out (i.e., in tears)" (Mowat, 36)

APEMANTUS

111 Ho, ho! I laugh to think that babe a bastard.

A bastard: "i.e. having no legitimate source" (Riverside, 1,498)

THIRD LORD

112 I promise you, my lord, you moved me much.

Promise: "assure" (Bevington)

APEMANTUS

113 Much!

Much: "a derisive exclamation" (Wright, 17)

Donald J. Richardson

Tucket, within

TIMON

114 What means that trump?

Enter a Servant

115 How now?

SERVANT

116 Please you, my lord, there are certain

117 ladies most desirous of admittance.

TIMON

118 Ladies! what are their wills?

SERVANT

119 There comes with them a forerunner, my lord, which

120 bears that office, to signify their pleasures.

TIMON

121 I pray, let them be admitted.

Enter Cupid

CUPID

122 Hail to thee, worthy Timon, and to all

123 That of his bounties taste! The five best senses

124 Acknowledge thee their patron; and come freely

Tucket: "trumpet call" (Riverside, 1,498)

Trump: "trumpet signal" (Mowat, 36)

What are their wills?: "i.e., **what** do they want" (Mowat, 36)

Forerunner: "herald, introducer" (Mowat, 36); **which . . . office**: "whose function is" (Riverside, 1,498)

Pleasures: "wishes" (Mowat, 36)

Enter Cupid: "i.e. as the presenter of the masque" (Riverside, 1,498); "i.e., a boy dressed as the Roman god of love" (Mowat, 36)

125 To gratulate thy plenteous bosom: there,

Gratulate: "salute";
plenteous: "generous";
there: "Most editors adopt
Theobald's emendation
Th'ear, and in line 126,
many emend *all* to *smell*
(following Theobald) or
read *smell, all* (following
Steevens)." (Riverside,
1,498); **plenteous bosom**:
"i.e., bountiful heart"
(Mowat, 36)

126 Taste, touch, all, pleas'd from thy tale rise;

127 They only now come but to feast thine eyes.

They: "i.e. the maskers"
(Riverside, 1,498);
only . . . but: "i.e., **now
come only**" (Mowat,
36); **but . . . eyes**: "i.e.,
only to appeal to the
sense of sight, whereas at
Timon's banquet all the
senses were gratified"
(Charney, 60)

TIMON

128 They're welcome all; let 'em have kind
admittance:

129 Music, make their welcome!

Music: "i.e., let music"
(Charney, 60)

Exit Cupid

FIRST LORD

130 You see, my lord, how ample you're beloved.

Ample: "fully"
(Williams, 18)

Music. Re-enter Cupid with a mask of Ladies as Amazons, with lutes in their hands, dancing and playing

Masque: an elaborate allegorical show or entertainment with emphasis on spectacle, music, and dance" (Charney, 60); **Amazons**: "members of a mythological tribe of female warriors, reputed to have lived in Scythia, near the Black Sea" (Mowat, 36)

APEMANTUS

131 Hoy-day, what a sweep of vanity comes this way!

Hoy-day: "a exclamation calling attention to something"; **vanity**: "This could mean, for example, 'worthlessness,' 'futility,' 'triviality,' and 'folly,' as well as 'conceit and desire for admiration.' All of these may be intended here." (Mowat, 36); **sweep**: "(in reference to the sweeping motion of the dancers)" (Charney, 60)

132 They dance! they are mad women.

133 Like madness is the glory of this life.

Like madness . . . root: "i.e., a similar **madness** is the splendor **of this life**, as is shown in the contrast between the **pomp** of this celebration and life's bare necessities" (Mowat, 38); **Like**: "similar"; **glory**: "vainglory, ostentation" (Riverside, 1,498)

134 As this pomp shows to a little oil and root.

As ... root: "as the magnificence of this feast shows itself to be in comparison with the basic necessities" (Riverside, 1,498)

135 We make ourselves fools, to disport ourselves;

Disport: "entertain" (Bevington)

136 And spend our flatteries, to drink those men

Drink: "(1) drink the health of; (2) consume (cf. *eats* in line 42 above and *eat* in I.i.232)" (Riverside, 1,499)

137 Upon whose age we void it up again,

Upon whose age: "i.e., **upon** whom, when they grow old"; **void**: "vomit" (Mowat, 38)

138 With poisonous spite and envy.

Envy: "malice" (Riverside, 1,499)

139 Who lives that's not depraved or depraves?

Depraved: "disparaged, vilified" (Mowat, 38); **depraves**: "slanders" (Bevington); "vilifies" (Williams, 18)

140 Who dies, that bears not one spurn to their graves

Spurn: "blow, injury" (Riverside, 1,499); "insult" (Charney, 60)

141 Of their friends' gift?

Gift: "giving" (Riverside, 1,499)

142 I should fear those that dance before me now

143 Would one day stamp upon me: 't has been done;

144 Men shut their doors against a setting sun.

Men ... setting sun: "Proverbial: 'The rising not the **setting, sun** is worshipped by most **men**.'" (Mowat, 38)

Donald J. Richardson

The Lords rise from table, with much adoring of TIMON; and to show their
loves, each singles out an Amazon, and all dance, men with women, a lofty
strain or two to the hautboys, and cease

Adoring: "reverential
saluting" (Riverside,
1,499); **hautboys**:
"oboelike instruments"
(Bevington)

TIMON

145 You have done our pleasures much grace, fair
    ladies,

Done our . . . grace:
"added much charm to our
pleasure" (Wright, 19)

146 Set a fair fashion on our entertainment,

Set . . . on: "i.e.,
beautifully enhanced"
(Mowat, 38)

147 Which was not half so beautiful and kind;

Was not: "i.e., **was not**
before you came" (Mowat,
38); **kind**: "gracious"
(Riverside, 1,499)

148 You have added worth unto 't and lustre,

149 And entertain'd me with mine own device;

Mine own device: "this
allegorical entertainment
which you have composed
especially for me (?).
Less probably, Timon
may be acknowledging
that he himself devised
the entertainment."
(Riverside, 1,499)

150 I am to thank you for 't.

Am to: "must" (Wright, 19)

FIRST LADY

151 My lord, you take us even at the best.

Take . . . best: "rate us
at the most favorable
valuation" (Riverside,
1,499)

APEMANTUS

152 'Faith, for the worst is filthy; and would not hold

Worst: "i.e., **worst** part" (Mowat, 38); **hold / taking**: "bear handling (being rotten)" (Riverside, 1,499)

153 taking, I doubt me.

Taking: "(wordplay . . . as sexually possessing implies that the lady has venereal disease)" (Mowat, 38); **doubt me**: "fear" (Riverside, 1,499)

TIMON

154 Ladies, there is an idle banquet attends you:

Idle: "trifling"; **banquet**: "dessert, refreshment" (Riverside, 1,499); **attends**: "awaits" (Mowat, 38)

155 Please you to dispose yourselves.

Dispose yourselves: "take your places" (Riverside, 1,499)

ALL LADIES

156 Most thankfully, my lord.

Exeunt Cupid and Ladies

TIMON

157 Flavius.

FLAVIUS

158 My lord?

TIMON

159 The little casket bring me hither.

FLAVIUS

160 Yes, my lord. More jewels yet!

161 There is no crossing him in 's humor;   **Crossing**: "opposing"; **humor**: "inclination, caprice" (Riverside, 1,499)

162 [*Aside*] Else I should tell him well (i' faith I should), **Well**: "forthrightly" (Riverside, 1,499)

163 When all's spent, he 'ld be cross'd then, and he could.   **He'ld be cross'd**: "he'd like to have his debts cancelled"; **and**: "if" (Riverside, 1,499)

164 'Tis pity bounty had not eyes behind,   **Had . . . behind**: "i.e., was not prudent or cautious (literally, did not have **eyes** at the back of the head)" (Mowat, 40); "could not see the consequences of its action" (Wright, 19)

165 That man might ne'er be wretched for his mind.   **For his mind**: "i.e. because of his generous impulses" (Riverside, 1,499)

Exit

FIRST LORD

166 Where be our men?

SERVANT

167 Here, my lord, in readiness.

SECOND LORD

168 Our horses!

Re-enter FLAVIUS, with the casket

TIMON

169 O my friends,

170 I have one word to say to you: look you, my good lord,

171 I must entreat you honor me so much   **You honor**: "you to honor" (Bevington)

172 As to advance this jewel; accept it and wear it,

Advance: "increase the value of (by accepting)" (Riverside, 1,499)

173 Kind my lord.

FIRST LORD

174 I am so far already in your gifts--

Am so far already in: "i.e., **already** have **so** many of" (Mowat, 40)

ALL

175 So are we all.

Enter a Servant

SERVANT

176 My lord, there are certain nobles of the senate

177 Newly alighted, and come to visit you.

TIMON

178 They are fairly welcome.

Fairly: "courteously. In line 188 the word may include the implication that the gift will be handsomely rewarded; cf. line 196, 'Not without fair reward.'" (Riverside, 1,499); "entirely" (Mowat, 40)

FLAVIUS

179 I beseech your honor,

180 Vouchsafe me a word; it does concern you near.

Vouchsafe: "allow" (Hinman, 50); **near**: "closely" (Mowat, 40)

TIMON

181 Near! why then, another time I'll hear thee:

Near . . . thee: "Compare *Julius Caesar* 3.1.6-8 : 'O Caesar, read mine first, for mine's a suit/ That touches Caesar nearer. . . . CAESAR What touches ourself shall be last served.'" (Mowat, 40)

182 I prithee, let's be provided to show them

183 entertainment.

FLAVIUS

184 [Aside] I scarce know how.

Enter a Second Servant

SECOND SERVANT

185 May it please your honor, Lord Lucius,

186 Out of his free love, hath presented to you

Out of his free love: "because of his abundant affection" (Wright, 20)

187 Four milk-white horses, trapp'd in silver.

Trapp'd in silver: "wearing silver- mounted trappings" (Riverside, 1,499); "(A *trapping* is a cloth or covering spread over the harness or saddle of a horse.)" (Mowat, 42)

TIMON

188 I shall accept them fairly; let the presents

Fairly: "courteously" (Mowat, 42)

189 Be worthily entertain'd.

Worthily entertain'd: "fittingly received" (Riverside, 1,499)

Enter a third Servant

190 How now! what news?

THIRD SERVANT

191 Please you, my lord, that honorable

192 gentleman, Lord Lucullus, entreats your company

193 to-morrow to hunt with him, and has sent your honor

194 two brace of greyhounds.　　　　**Brace**: "pair" (Bevington)

TIMON

195 I'll hunt with him; and let them be received,

196 Not without fair reward.　　　　**Fair reward**: "a generous tip to the servant who brings them" (Wright, 21)

FLAVIUS

197 [Aside] What will this come to?　　　　**Come to**: "result in" (Wright, 21)

198 He commands us to provide, and give great gifts,

199 And all out of an empty coffer:

200 Nor will he know his purse, or yield me this,　　　　**Purse**: "financial situation" (Bevington); **yield me this**: "i.e., provide me with the opportunity" (Mowat, 42)

201 To show him what a beggar his heart is,　　　　**What ... is**: "cf. the proverb 'Unhappy he who cannot do the good that he would.'" (Wright, 21)

202 Being of no power to make his wishes good:　　　　**Being of**: "i.e., the desires of his heart having" (Bevington)

203 His promises fly so beyond his state　　　　**State**: "estate, means" (Riverside, 1,499)

204 That what he speaks is all in debt; he owes

205 For every word: he is so kind that he now

206 Pays interest for 't; his land's put to their books. **Put . . . books**: "i.e. mortgaged to the very people to whom he makes gifts" (Riverside, 1,499)

207 Well, would I were gently put out of office

208 Before I were forced out!

209 Happier is he that has no friend to feed

210 Than such that do e'en enemies exceed. **Than . . . exceed**: "than he who has such friends as do him more harm than enemies" (Riverside, 1,499)

211 I bleed inwardly for my lord.

Exit

TIMON

212 You do yourselves

213 Much wrong, you bate too much of your own merits: **Bate . . . of**: "undervalue too much" (Riverside, 1,499)

214 Here, my lord, a trifle of our love.

SECOND LORD

215 With more than common thanks I will receive it.

THIRD LORD

216 O, he's the very soul of bounty!

TIMON

217 And now I remember, my lord, you gave **Gave / Good words**: "i.e., spoke complimentarily" (Mowat, 44)

218 Good words the other day of a bay courser **Courser**: "stallion, or swift horse" (Mowat, 44)

219 I rode on: it is yours, because you liked it.

SECOND LORD

220 O, I beseech you, pardon me, my lord, in that.

Pardon . . . that: "i.e., permit me to decline that too generous gift" (Riverside, 1,499)

TIMON

221 You may take my word, my lord; I know, no man

222 Can justly praise but what he does affect:

But: "anything except" (Hinman, 52); **affect**: "like" (Riverside, 1,500)

223 I weigh my friend's affection with mine own;

Weigh . . . with: "regard my friend's wishes as equal in importance to" (Riverside, 1,500)

224 I'll tell you true. I'll call to you.

I'll . . . true: "believe me" (Wright, 22); **to**: "on" (Riverside, 1,500)

ALL LORDS

225 O, none so welcome.

TIMON

226 I take all and your several visitations

All . . . several: "your joint and individual" (Riverside, 1,500); **visitations**: "visits" (Williams, 22)

227 So kind to heart, 'tis not enough to give;

Kind: "i.e., kindly"; **'tis . . . give**: "i.e., that there is not **enough** in my possession to meet my desire **to give**" (Mowat, 44)

228 Methinks, I could deal kingdoms to my friends,

Deal: "distribute" (Charney, 64)

229 And ne'er be weary. Alcibiades,

230 Thou art a soldier, therefore seldom rich;

231 It comes in charity to thee: for all thy living

It: "what you receive, a gift" (Charney, 64); **It . . . thee**: "to give to you is genuine charity" (Riverside, 1,500); **living**: "(1) life, existence; (2) means of making a **living**; (3) lands" (Mowat, 44)

232 Is 'mongst the dead, and all the lands thou hast

233 Lie in a pitch'd field.

Pitch'd field: "battlefield" (Riverside, 1,500)

ALCIBIADES

234 Ay, defil'd land, my lord.

Defil'd: "a quibble on *pitch'd* ('He that touches pitch shall be defiled,' Ecclesiasticus 13:1); perhaps also playing on *filed* = with soldiers drawn up in ranks" (Riverside, 1,500)

FIRST LORD

235 We are so virtuously bound--

Bound: "under obligation" (Williams, 22)

TIMON

236 And so

237 Am I to you.

SECOND LORD

238 So infinitely endear'd--

Endear'd: "obligated" (Wright, 22)

TIMON

239 All to you. Lights, more lights!

All to you: "i.e., the obligation is entirely mine; or, all mine is yours" (Bevington)

FIRST LORD

240 The best of happiness,

241 Honor and fortunes, keep with you, Lord Timon!   **Keep**: "dwell, remain" (Bevington)

TIMON

242 Ready for his friends.   **Ready for**: "ready to assist" (Bevington)

Exeunt all but APEMANTUS and TIMON

APEMANTUS

243 What a coil's here!   **Coil**: "fuss" (Riverside, 1,500)

244 Serving of becks and jutting-out of bums!   **Serving of becks**: "bowing" (Riverside, 1,500); **Jutting-out of bums**: "bowings" (Wright, 23); **bums**: "posteriors" (Charney, 65)

245 I doubt whether their legs be worth the sums   **Legs**: "(1) limbs; (2) bows" (Riverside, 1,500)

246 That are given for 'em. Friendship's full of dregs: **Dregs**: "corruption; probably with thought of the proverb 'There is fraud in friendship.'" (Wright, 23)

247 Methinks, false hearts should never have sound legs,   **Sound**: "i.e. able to make bows" (Riverside, 1,500)

248 Thus honest fools lay out their wealth on court'sies.   **Lay out**: "spend"; **court'sies**: "(1) curtsies, or bows; (2) courtesies" (Mowat, 46); **on**: "in exchange for" (Wright, 23)

TIMON

249 Now, Apemantus, if thou wert not sullen, I would be   **Sullen**: "obstinate" (Wright, 23)

250 good to thee.

APEMANTUS

251 No, I'll nothing: for if I should be bribed too,   **I'll nothing**: "i.e.,
I'll accept **nothing**"
(Mowat, 46)

252 there would be none left to rail upon thee, and then   **Rail upon**: "revile"
(Charney, 65)

253 thou wouldst sin the faster. Thou givest so long,   **Long**: "largely"
(Wright, 23)

254 Timon, I fear me thou wilt give away thyself in   **Fear me**: "i.e., **fear**"
(Mowat, 46); **in / paper**:
"i.e. in promissory notes
because there are no
valuables left" (Riverside,
1,500)

255 paper shortly: what needs these feasts, pomps and   **What needs**: "what
necessity is there for"
(Bevington)

256 vain-glories?

TIMON

257 Nay, and you begin to rail on society once, I am   **And . . . once**: "if once
you begin to attack
friendly companionship"
(Riverside, 1,500)

258 sworn not to give regard to you. Farewell; and   **Give regard**: "to take
     come   notice of" (Bevington)

259 with better music.   **With better music**:
"i.e., when you can sing
another song (proverbial)"
(Mowat, 46)

Exit

APEMANTUS

260 So; thou wilt not hear me now, thou shalt

So: "very well" (Riverside, 1,500); **thou**: "i.e., if you" (Mowat, 46); **thou . . . then**: "you will not be able to listen to me later, when you are bankrupt" (Charney, 65)

261 not then. I'll lock thy heaven from thee.

Thy heaven: "i.e. my saving advice" (Riverside, 1,500)

262 O, that men's ears should be

263 To counsel deaf, but not to flattery!

Exit

ACT II

SCENE I. A Senator's house.

Enter Senator, with papers in his hand

SENATOR

1 And late, five thousand: to Varro and to Isidore

Late: "recently" (Mowat, 50); **five thousand**: "(presumably 'crowns' as in III,iv,29; a very large sum is evidently meant)" (Hinman, 54)

2 He owes nine thousand; besides my former sum,

3 Which makes it five and twenty. Still in motion

Still in motion / Of raging waste: "still pursuing a course of headlong extravagance" (Wright, 24)

4 Of raging waste? It cannot hold; it will not.

Hold: "last" (Riverside, 1,500)

5 If I want gold, steal but a beggar's dog,

Steal: "I need only steal" (Riverside, 1,500)

6 And give it Timon, why, the dog coins gold.

7 If I would sell my horse, and buy twenty more

8 Better than he, why, give my horse to Timon,

9 Ask nothing, give it him, it foals me straight,

Foals me: "figuratively, produces for me" (Wright, 24); **straight**: "immediately" (Charney, 66)

10 And able horses. No porter at his gate,

Able horses: "i.e. not foals, either, but full-grown horses"; **porter**: "i.e. one who keeps people out" (Riverside, 1,500)

11 But rather one that smiles and still invites

Still: "always" (Mowat, 50)

12 All that pass by. It cannot hold: no reason

Hold: "continue" (Williams, 24); **reason**: "i.e. rational person" (Riverside, 1,500)

13 Can found his state in safety. Caphis, ho!

Sound . . . safety: "i.e. estimate his estate as safe" (Riverside, 1,500)

14 Caphis, I say!

Enter CAPHIS

CAPHIS

15 Here, sir; what is your pleasure?

SENATOR

16 Get on your cloak, and haste you to Lord Timon;

17 Importune him for my moneys; be not ceas'd

Ceas'd: "put off" (Riverside, 1,500)

18 With slight denial, nor then silenced when—

When . . . thus: "i.e., when you are greeted with polite subservience (to remove one's **cap**—so that it **plays in the right hand thus**—was a mark of respect to a social superior and thus an act of subservience to a social equal, as Caphis would be to one of Timon's servants.)" (Mowat, 50)

19 "Commend me to your master"--and the cap

"Commend me . . ." . . . thus: "(examples of anticipated ceremonious delays by Timon)" (Charney, 67)

20 Plays in the right hand, thus: but tell him,

21 My uses cry to me, I must serve my turn

Uses: "needs, business undertakings" (Riverside, 1,500)

22 Out of mine own; his days and times are past

Out of mine own: "with my own money" (Wright, 25); **his . . . past**: "the terms of his loans have expired" (Riverside, 1,500); **days and times**: "i.e., the **days and times** specified for his repayments" (Mowat, 52)

23 And my reliances on his fracted dates

Fracted: "broken"; **dates**: "due dates for repayment (so also in line 36)" (Riverside, 1,500)

24 Have smit my credit: I love and honor him,

Smit: "damaged" (Riverside, 1,500)

25 But must not break my back to heal his finger;

26 Immediate are my needs, and my relief

27 Must not be toss'd and turn'd to me in words,

Toss'd and turn'd: "hit back to me (metaphor from tennis" (Riverside, 1,500)

28 But find supply immediate. Get you gone:

29 Put on a most importunate aspect,

Aspect: "accent on second syllable" (Mowat, 52)

30 A visage of demand; for, I do fear,

31 When every feather sticks in his own wing,

Every . . . wing: "i.e. every creditor has taken what is due him" (Riverside, 1,500)

32 Lord Timon will be left a naked gull,

Gull: "(1) unfledged bird; (2) dupe, fool" (Riverside, 1,500)

33 Which flashes now a phoenix. Get you gone.

Which: "i.e., who"; **phoenix**: "mythical bird, only one of which was alive at a single time—a rare and precious creature" (Mowat, 52)

CAPHIS

34 I go, sir.

SENATOR

35 "I go, sir!"--Take the bonds along with you,

36 And have the dates in. Come.

Have the dates in: "i.e., mark the due dates, rather than just the periods (e.g., six months), on **the bonds** so that it is obvious that they are overdue (Many editors emend 'in. Come' to 'in compt,' which means 'reckoned.')" (Mowat, 52)

CAPHIS

37 I will, sir.

SENATOR

38 Go.

Exeunt

SCENE II. The same. A hall in Timon's house.

Enter FLAVIUS, with many bills in his hand

FLAVIUS

1 No care, no stop! so senseless of expense,

Senseless: "unmindful" (Mowat, 52)

2 That he will neither know how to maintain it,

Know: "find out" (Riverside, 1,501)

3 Nor cease his flow of riot. Takes no accompt

Riot: "extravagant reveling"; **accompt**: "account" (Riverside, 1,501); **takes**: "i.e., he **takes**" (Mowat, 52)

4 How things go from him, nor

5 resumes no care

Resumes . . . continue: "i.e. assumes any responsibility to provide what he needs **to continue** (his extravagance)" (Mowat, 52)

6 Of what is to continue: never mind

What is to continue: "what remains in possession" (Wright, 26); **never . . . kind**: "i.e., there was **never** a **mind** so **unwise** in being **so kind**" (Mowat, 54)

7 Was to be so unwise, to be so kind.

Was to be: "was fated to be"; **to be**: "as to be (?) or in being (?)" (Riverside, 1,501)

8 What shall be done? he will not hear, till feel:

Hear, till feel: "listen to warnings till the actual disaster befalls him" (Williams, 25)

9 I must be round with him, now he comes from hunting.

Round: "plain, blunt" (Riverside, 1,501)

10 Fie, fie, fie, fie!

Enter CAPHIS, and the Servants of Isidore and Varro

CAPHIS

11 Good even, Varro: what,

> **Good even**: "i.e., **good** afternoon (**Even** refers to any time after noon.)"; **Varro**: "i.e., Varro's servant"; **what**: "an interjection introducing a question" (Mowat, 54)

12 You come for money?

VARRO'S SERVANT

13 Is't not your business too?

CAPHIS

14 It is: and yours too, Isidore?

ISIDORE'S SERVANT

15 It is so.

CAPHIS

16 Would we were all discharg'd!

> **Discharg'd**: "paid" (Riverside, 1,501)

VARRO'S SERVANT

17 I fear it.

> **I fear it**: "i.e. I'm afraid we won't be" (Riverside, 1,501)

CAPHIS

18 Here comes the lord.

Enter TIMON, ALCIBIADES, and Lords, & c

TIMON

19 So soon as dinner's done, we'll forth again,

> **Dinner's**: "Dinner was the noontime meal."; **forth**: "i.e., go out" (Mowat, 54)

20 My Alcibiades. With me? what is your will?

CAPHIS

21 My lord, here is a note of certain dues.

TIMON

22 Dues! Whence are you?   **Dues**: "debts" (Mowat, 54)

CAPHIS

23 Of Athens here, my lord.

TIMON

24 Go to my steward.

CAPHIS

25 Please it your lordship, he hath put me off

26 To the succession of new days this month: **To . . . month**: "i.e. from one day to the next for the past month" (Riverside, 1,501)

27 My master is awak'd by great occasion   **Awak'd . . . occasion**: "aroused by great needs which have arisen" (Riverside, 1,501)

28 To call upon his own, and humbly prays you   **His own**: "i.e. what is rightfully due him" (Riverside, 1,501)

29 That with your other noble parts you'll suit   **With . . . suit**: "you will act like your noble self" (Wright, 27); **parts**: "endowments" (Williams, 26); **suit**: "be consistent" (Riverside, 1,501)

30 In giving him his right.

TIMON

31 Mine honest friend,

32 I prithee, but repair to me next morning.

But: "only" (Williams, 26); **repair**: "return" (Mowat, 54)

CAPHIS

33 Nay, good my lord--

TIMON

34 Contain thyself, good friend.

VARRO'S SERVANT

35 One Varro's servant, my good lord--

ISIDORE'S SERVANT

36 From Isidore;

37 He humbly prays your speedy payment.

CAPHIS

38 If you did know, my lord, my master's wants—

Wants: "needs" (Mowat, 56)

VARRO'S SERVANT

39 'Twas due on forfeiture, my lord, six weeks

On forfeiture: "under penalty of forfeit for non-payment on due date" (Riverside, 1,501); **six weeks / And past**: "more than six weeks ago" (Wright, 27)

40 And past.

ISIDORE'S SERVANT

41 Your steward puts me off, my lord;

42 And I am sent expressly to your lordship.

TIMON

43 Give me breath.

Breath: "i.e., room to breathe" (Mowat, 56)

44 I do beseech you, good my lords, keep on;

Keep on: "go on ahead" (Riverside, 1,501)

45 I'll wait upon you instantly.

Wait . . . instantly: "i.e., be back in your company immediately" (Mowat, 56)

Exeunt ALCIBIADES and Lords

To FLAVIUS

46 Come hither: pray you,

47 How goes the world, that I am thus encounter'd

How . . . world: "what on earth is going on" (Riverside, 1,501)

48 With clamorous demands of debt, broken bonds,

Debt, broken: "Some editors omit *debt*, in view of the metrical irregularity and the occurrence of *debts* in line 49; others, following Steevens, read *date-broke*, i.e. overdue." (Riverside, 1,501)

49 And the detention of long-since-due debts,

Detention: "non-payment" (Riverside, 1,501); "withholding" (Mowat, 56)

50 Against my honor

Against: "to the detriment of" (Riverside, 1,501)

FLAVIUS

51 Please you, gentlemen,

52 The time is unagreeable to this business:

Unagreeable: "unsuitable" (Williams, 27)

53 Your importunacy cease till after dinner,

Importunacy: "i.e., persistence in making demands" (Mowat, 56)

54 That I may make his lordship understand

That: "i.e., so **that**" (Mowat, 56)

55 Wherefore you are not paid.

Wherefore: "why" (Mowat, 56)

TIMON

56 Do so, my friends. See them well entertain'd.

Entertain'd: "received, treated" (Bevington)

Exit

FLAVIUS

57 Pray, draw near.

Pray, draw near: "This line may be directed to Timon or to the creditors' men." (Mowat, 56); "come this way" (Hinman, 57)

Exit

Enter APEMANTUS and Fool

Fool: "In the drama of Shakespeare's time, the Fool is usually a servant who makes his living by amusing his aristocratic patron. In this play, the Fool seems to serve a brothel-keeper." (Mowat, 56)

CAPHIS

58 Stay, stay, here comes the fool with Apemantus:

59 let's ha' some sport with 'em.

Ha': "have" (Bevington)

VARRO'S SERVANT

60 Hang him, he'll abuse us.

Abuse: "vilify" (Bevington)

ISIDORE'S SERVANT

61 A plague upon him, dog!

VARRO'S SERVANT

62 How dost, fool?

APEMANTUS

63 Dost dialogue with thy shadow?

VARRO'S SERVANT

64 I speak not to thee.

APEMANTUS

65 No,'tis to thyself.

'Tis to thyself: "you speak to yourself (when you say 'How dost, Fool?'). Apemantus thus calls Varro's servant a fool." (Riverside, 1,501)

To the Fool

66 Come away.

ISIDORE'S SERVANT

67 There's the fool hangs on your back already.

There's . . . already: "i.e., you have **already** had the name **fool** affixed to **your back**" (Mowat, 58)

APEMANTUS

68 No, thou stand'st single, th 'rt not on him yet.

Single: "by yourself"; **th' art . . . yet**: "i.e. you're not on his back yet. Apemantus thus calls Isidore's servant a fool." (Riverside, 1,501)

CAPHIS

69 Where's the fool now?

Where's . . . now: "i.e. whose back is the Fool on now" (Riverside, 1,501)

APEMANTUS

70 He last asked the question. Poor rogues, and

He . . . question: "Apemantus thus calls Caphis a fool." (Riverside, 1,501)

71 usurers' men! bawds between gold and want!

Usurers' men: "servants of those who collect interest when lending money, contrary to Christian teaching in Shakespeare's day"; **bawds**: "panders, go-betweens" (Mowat, 58)

ALL SERVANTS

72 What are we, Apemantus?

APEMANTUS

73 Asses.

ALL SERVANTS

74 Why?

APEMANTUS

75 That you ask me what you are, and do not know

Do not know / yourselves: "compare the proverb 'He is a fool that forgets himself.'" (Wright, 29)

76 yourselves. Speak to 'em, fool.

FOOL

77 How do you, gentlemen?

ALL SERVANTS

78 Gramercies, good fool: how does your mistress?

Gramercies: "many thanks" (Riverside, 1,501)

FOOL

79 She's e'en setting on water to scald such chickens

Scald: "a method of removing feathers from poultry. The Fool alludes to loss of hair from venereal disease and to its treatment by 'sweating.' His mistress is a bawd or a prostitute." (Riverside, 1,501)

80 as you are. Would we could see you at Corinth!

Corinth: "brothel, or brothel district. (The city of Corinth was notorious for prostitutes.)" (Riverside, 1,501)

APEMANTUS

81 Good! gramercy.

Enter Page

FOOL

82 Look you, here comes my master's page.

Master's: "Many editors read *mistress'*, following Theobald, but the Fool and the Page could have had both a master and a mistress; cf. Boult in *Pericles*, who calls the Pander master and the Bawd mistress (IV.vi.147-48)." (Riverside, 1,501)

PAGE

83 [To the Fool] Why, how now, captain! what do you

Captain: "a familiar term of address" (Williams, 28)

84 in this wise company? How dost thou, Apemantus?

APEMANTUS

85 Would I had a rod in my mouth, that I might answer

Rod: "stick (to beat you with)" (Mowat, 58); **answer / thee profitably**: "i.e. chastise you with my words to your profit" (Riverside, 1,502)

86 thee profitably.

Profitably: "i.e., for your benefit (by teaching you a lesson)" (Mowat, 58)

PAGE

87 Prithee, Apemantus, read me the superscription of

Superscription of: "i.e., addresses on" (Mowat, 58)

88 these letters: I know not which is which.

APEMANTUS

89 Canst not read?

PAGE

90 No.

APEMANTUS

91 There will little learning die then, that day thou

92 art hanged. This is to Lord Timon; this to

93 Alcibiades. Go; thou wast born a bastard, and thou't

Thou't: "thou wilt" (Riverside, 1,502)

94 die a bawd.

PAGE

95 Thou wast whelped a dog, and thou shalt famish a

Whelped: "born (literally, brought forth as a whelp or puppy)"; **famish . . . death**: "starve to **death** like a **dog**" (Mowat, 60)

96 dog's death. Answer not; I am gone.

Exit

APEMANTUS

97 E'en so thou outrun'st grace. Fool, I will go with

E'en so: "precisely so" (Bevington); **thou outrun'st grace**: "i.e. you flee from the instruction that might save you (cf. I.ii.261)" (Riverside, 1,502)

98 you to Lord Timon's.

FOOL

99 Will you leave me there?

APEMANTUS

100 If Timon stay at home. You three serve three usurers?

If . . . home: "i.e. if I leave Timon there, I'll leave a fool there" (Riverside, 1,502); **You three**: "do you three" (Bevington)

ALL SERVANTS

101 Ay; would they served us!

Would: "i.e., we wish" (Mowat, 60)

APEMANTUS

102 So would I--as good a trick as ever hangman served thief.

FOOL

103 Are you three usurers' men?

ALL SERVANTS

104 Ay, fool.

FOOL

105 I think no usurer but has a fool to his servant: my

I . . . servant: "implying that any servant to a usurer is a fool" (Riverside, 1,502)

106 mistress is one, and I am her fool. When men come

One: "not a usurer, apparently, but a brothel-keeper, like the Fool's master, whose effect on his customers the Fool then compares to a usurer's (lines 106-07) In *Measure for Measure* 3.2.5, fornication and moneylending are called 'two usuries.' And line 71, above, compares 'usurers' men' to 'bawds.'" (Mowat, 60)

107 to borrow of your masters, they approach sadly, and

Sadly: "gravely" (Charney, 72)

108 go away merry; but they enter my mistress' house

109 merrily, and go away sadly: the reason of this?

VARRO'S SERVANT

110 I could render one.

One: "(for instance that they are now poorer— and probably diseased as well)" (Hinman, 59)

APEMANTUS

111 Do it then, that we may account thee a whoremaster

112 and a knave; which not-withstanding, thou shalt be

113 no less esteem'd.

No less esteem'd: "a slur at Athenian morals" (Riverside, 1,502)

VARRO'S SERVANT

114 What is a whoremaster, fool?

FOOL

115 A fool in good clothes, and something like thee.

116 'Tis a spirit: sometime't appears like a lord;

A spirit: "i.e., a being capable of shifting its shape" (Mowat, 60)

117 sometime like a lawyer; sometime like a philosopher,

Sometime: "at times" (Williams, 29)

118 with two stones moe than's artificial one: he is

Stones: "testicles"; **artificial one**: "i.e. the philosopher's stone (alchemical)" (Riverside, 1,502); **than's**: "than his, the philosopher's" (Bevington)

119 very often like a knight; and, generally, in all

120 shapes that man goes up and down in from fourscore

121 to thirteen, this spirit walks in.

VARRO'S SERVANT

122 Thou art not altogether a fool.

FOOL

123 Nor thou altogether a wise man: as much foolery as

124 I have, so much wit thou lackest.

APEMANTUS

125 That answer might have become Apemantus.

Become: "been a credit to" (Wright, 30)

ALL SERVANTS

126 Aside, aside; here comes Lord Timon.

Re-enter TIMON and FLAVIUS

APEMANTUS

127 Come with me, fool, come.

FOOL

128 I do not always follow lover, elder brother and

Lover . . . / woman: "types of people proverbially represented as fools" (Mowat, 62); **elder brother**: "i.e. the son who inherits; and so, like lovers and women, the most profitable kind of person for the Fool to cultivate" (Riverside, 1,502)

129 woman; sometime the philosopher.

Exeunt APEMANTUS and Fool

FLAVIUS

130 Pray you, walk near: I'll speak with you anon.

Walk near: "i.e., stay close by"; **anon**: "soon" (Mowat, 62)

Exeunt Servants

TIMON

131 You make me marvel: wherefore ere this time

Wherefore: "why" (Mowat, 62)

132 Had you not fully laid my state before me,

Fully . . . state: "completely detailed my financial position" (Bevington)

133 That I might so have rated my expense,

Rated: "estimated" (Riverside, 1,502); "allotted" (Williams, 30)

134 As I had leave of means?

As . . . means: "in accordance with my resources" (Riverside, 1,502)

FLAVIUS

135 You would not hear me,

136 At many leisures I propos'd.

At many leisures: "i.e., many a time when you were unoccupied" (Mowat, 62); **propos'd**: "attempted (to tell you)" (Riverside, 1,502)

TIMON

137 Go to!

Go to: "exclamation of impatience or indignation" (Riverside, 1,502)

138 Perchance some single vantages you took.

Single vantages: "particular opportunities" (Mowat, 62)

139 When my indisposition put you back:

Indisposition: "disinclination to listen" (Riverside, 1,502)

140 And that unaptness made your minister,

That . . . yourself: "you used my unwillingness to listen on those few occasions as an excuse for not trying again" (Riverside, 1,502); **minister**: "i.e., means" (Mowat, 62)

141 Thus to excuse yourself.

FLAVIUS

142 O my good lord,

143 At many times I brought in my accounts,

144 Laid them before you; you would throw them off,

145 And say, you found them in mine honesty.

Found . . . honesty: "i.e., found warrant for believing the books properly kept in knowing me to be honest" (Bevington)

146 When, for some trifling present, you have bid me

147 Return so much, I have shook my head and wept;

So much: "i.e., **so much** more than the **present** was worth" (Mowat, 62)

148 Yea, 'gainst the authority of manners, pray'd you

'Gainst . . . manners: "contrary to what good manners required" (Riverside, 1,502)

149 To hold your hand more close: I did endure

Hold . . . close: "i.e., spend less" (Mowat, 62)

150 Not seldom, nor no slight checks, when I have

Seldom: "infrequent"; **checks**: "rebukes" (Riverside, 1,502)

151 Prompted you in the ebb of your estate

Prompted you: "told you what you ought to do"; **in**: "in the matter of" (Riverside, 1,502); "i.e., during" (Mowat, 62)

152 And your great flow of debts. My loved lord,

153 Though you hear now, too late--yet now's a time--

A time: "i.e. a time at least to tell you" (Riverside, 1,502)

154 The greatest of your having lacks a half

The greatest . . . having: "your possessions at the most sanguine estimate" (Riverside, 1,502); **lacks a half**: "i.e., is not enough by **a half**" (Mowat, 62)

155 To pay your present debts.

TIMON

156 Let all my land be sold.

FLAVIUS

157 'Tis all engag'd, some forfeited and gone;

Engag'd: "mortgaged" (Riverside, 1,502)

158 And what remains will hardly stop the mouth

Stop / Of: "satisfy" (Bevington)

159 Of present dues: the future comes apace:

Present dues: "debts now due" (Riverside, 1,502); **apace**: "quickly" (Bevington)

160 What shall defend the interim? and at length

What . . . interim: "i.e. what preparation can we make against the onslaught of debts that will be coming due in the near future"; **at length**: "in the long run" (Riverside, 1,502)

161 How goes our reckoning?

TIMON

162 To Lacedaemon did my land extend.

Lacedaemon: "Sparta" (Riverside, 1,502)

FLAVIUS

163 O my good lord, the world is but a word:

164 Were it all yours to give it in a breath,

165 How quickly were it gone!

TIMON

166 You tell me true.

FLAVIUS

167 If you suspect my husbandry or falsehood,

My . . . falsehood: "i.e. that my management has been dishonest. Some editors emend *or* to *of*." (Riverside, 1,502)

168 Call me before the exactest auditors

169 And set me on the proof. So the gods bless me,

Set . . . proof: "subject me to the test" (Mowat, 64); **on**: "to" (Riverside, 1,502)

170 When all our offices have been oppress'd

Offices: "kitchens and other service departments"; **oppress'd**: "taxed to the limit" (Riverside, 1,502)

171 With riotous feeders, when our vaults have wept

With: "by, because of" (Riverside, 1,502) **riotous**: "reveling"; **feeders**: "those who eat at the expense of others; dependents (a contemptuous term)"; **vaults**: "wine cellars (but **vaults** also could mean 'drains')" (Mowat, 64)

172 With drunken spilth of wine, when every room

Spilth: "spilling" (Riverside, 1,502)

173 Hath blazed with lights and bray'd with minstrelsy,

Bray'd: "resounded noisily" (Riverside, 1,503); **ministrelsy**: "playing and singing" (Mowat, 64)

174 I have retir'd me to a wasteful cock,

Retir'd . . . flow: "i.e. withdrawn to sit beside one of the flowing barrels and added my tears to its waste" (Riverside, 1,503); **wasteful cock**: "spigot (of a wine cask) that has not been shut off" (Charney, 75)

175 And set mine eyes at flow.

And . . . flow: "i.e., following the example of the 'wasteful cock,' I have added my tears to the general riot and superfluity" (Charney, 75)

TIMON

176 Prithee, no more.

FLAVIUS

177 Heavens, have I said, the bounty of this lord!

178 How many prodigal bits have slaves and peasants

Prodigal bits: "lavishly provided delicacies" (Riverside, 1,503)

179 This night englutted! Who is not Timon's?

Englutted: "gulped down" (Charney, 75); **who is not Timon's**: "i.e., **who** does not profess himself entirely devoted to Timon" (Mowat, 64)

180 What heart, head, sword, force, means, but is

Means: "financial resources" (Bevington)

181 Lord Timon's?

182 Great Timon, noble, worthy, royal Timon!

183 Ah, when the means are gone that buy this praise,

184 The breath is gone whereof this praise is made:

185 Feast-won, fast-lost; one cloud of winter showers,

Feast-won, fast-lost: "i.e., anything achieved by giving feasts is quickly lost (with wordplay on **fast** as a period of abstaining from food— the opposite of **feast**)" (Mowat, 64)

186 These flies are couch'd.

Are couch'd: "go into hiding" (Riverside 1,503)

TIMON

187 Come, sermon me no further:

Sermon me: "i.e., preach to **me**" (Mowat, 64)

188 No villainous bounty yet hath pass'd my heart;

Villainous bounty: "generosity that I am ashamed of" (Bevington)

189 Unwisely, not ignobly, have I given.

190 Why dost thou weep? Canst thou the conscience lack,

Conscience: "good sense, judgment" (Riverside 1,503)

191 To think I shall lack friends? Secure thy heart;

Secure: "set at ease" (Riverside 1,503)

192 If I would broach the vessels of my love,

Broach: "tap" (Riverside 1,503)

193 And try the argument of hearts by borrowing,

Try ... hearts: "test avowals of love" (Riverside 1,503); **argument**: "summary of subject-matter of a book, (figuratively) contents" (Williams, 32)

194 Men and men's fortunes could I frankly use

Frankly: "as freely" (Riverside 1,503)

195 As I can bid thee speak.

FLAVIUS

196 Assurance bless your thoughts!

Assurance ... thoughts: "may your hopes be blessed by proving well founded" (Riverside 1,503)

TIMON

197 And, in some sort, these wants of mine are crown'd,

Sort: "way" (Mowat, 66); **crown'd**: "given great dignity" (Riverside 1,503)

198 That I account them blessings; for by these

That: "so that" (Riverside 1,503)

199 Shall I try friends: you shall perceive how you

Try: "test" (Mowat, 66)

200 Mistake my fortunes; I am wealthy in my friends.

201 Within there! Flaminius! Servilius!

Enter FLAMINIUS, SERVILIUS, and other Servants

SERVANTS

202 My lord? my lord?

TIMON

203 I will dispatch you severally; you to Lord Lucius;   **Severally**: "individually, separately" (Mowat, 66)

204 to Lord Lucullus you: I hunted with his honor

205 to-day: you, to Sempronius: commend me to their

206 loves, and, I am proud, say, that my occasions have   **Occasions . . . time**: "needs . . . occasion" (Riverside 1,503)

207 found time to use 'em toward a supply of money: let   **Time**: "opportunity" (Bevington) ; **toward**: "i.e., for" (Mowat, 66)

208 the request be fifty talents.

FLAMINIUS

209 As you have said, my lord.

FLAVIUS

210 [Aside] Lord Lucius and Lucullus? hum!

TIMON

211 Go you, sir, to the senators--

212 Of whom, even to the state's best health, I have   **To . . . health**: "i.e. by my contributions to the welfare of the state" (Riverside 1,503)

213 Deserved this hearing--bid 'em send o' the instant   **O' the instant**: "at once" (Bevington)

214 A thousand talents to me.

Talents: "A talent was a huge sum of money. It is equal to nearly sixty pounds of silver, and by modern standards . . . about two thousand dollars." (Asimov, 138)

FLAVIUS

215 I have been bold--

216 For that I knew it the most general way—

For that: "because" (Mowat, 66); **general**: "usual (?) or comprehensive, i.e. offering the possibility of the largest loan (?)" (Riverside 1,503)

217 To them to use your signet and your name;

To them to use: "i.e., in going **to them** and in using" (Mowat, 66); **signet**: "seal (as proof of authority to act)" (Riverside 1,503)

218 But they do shake their heads, and I am here

219 No richer in return.

TIMON

220 Is't true? can't be?

FLAVIUS

221 They answer, in a joint and corporate voice,

Corporate: "united" (Mowat, 68)

222 That now they are at fall, want treasure, cannot

At fall: "at a low ebb"; **want treasure**: "lack funds" (Riverside 1,503)

223 Do what they would; are sorry--you are honorable--

224 But yet they could have wish'd--they know not--

225 Something hath been amiss--a noble nature

226 May catch a wrench--would all were well--'tis pity-- **Catch a wrench**: "suffer a twist from its proper direction" (Riverside 1,503)

227 And so, intending other serious matters, **Intending**: "pretending (?) or busying themselves with (?)" (Riverside 1,503)

228 After distasteful looks and these hard fractions, **Distasteful**: "indicating their distaste"; **hard fractions**: "harsh fragments of sentences" (Riverside 1,503)

229 With certain half-caps and cold-moving nods **Half-caps**: "grudging salutes"; **cold- moving**: "(1) stiff (as if with benumbed muscles); (2) importing coldness" (Riverside 1,503)

230 They froze me into silence.

TIMON

231 You gods, reward them!

232 Prithee, man, look cheerly. These old fellows **Cheerly**: "cheerful" (Mowat, 68)

233 Have their ingratitude in them hereditary:

234 Their blood is cak'd, 'tis cold, it seldom flows; **Cak'd**: "congealed. Old age was associated with the melancholy humor, described in the traditional physiology as dry and cold." (Riverside 1,503)

235 'Tis lack of kindly warmth they are not kind; **Lack**: "i.e. from lack" (Hinman, 64); **kindly**: "(1) natural; (2) friendly" (Mowat, 68)

236 And nature, as it grows again toward earth,

Earth: "i.e., the grave" (Mowat, 68)

237 Is fashion'd for the journey, dull and heavy.

To a Servant

238 Go to Ventidius.

To FLAVIUS

239 Prithee, be not sad,

240 Thou art true and honest; ingeniously I speak.

Ingeniously: "sincerely, unfeignedly" (Riverside 1,503)

241 No blame belongs to thee.

To Servant

242 Ventidius lately

243 Buried his father; by whose death he's stepp'd

244 Into a great estate: when he was poor,

When he was poor: "etc. (These lines echo Matthew 25:34-37 when Jesus discusses the Last Judgment.)" (Bevington)

245 Imprison'd and in scarcity of friends,

In scarcity of: "i.e., without" (Mowat, 68)

246 I clear'd him with five talents: greet him from me;

Clear'd him: "i.e., paid his debts and thereby released **him** from (debtors') prison" (Mowat, 68)

247 Bid him suppose some good necessity

Good necessity: "valid need" (Charney,77)

248 Touches his friend, which craves to be remember'd

Craves . . . talents: "i.e. asks that Vendidius recall the gift which restored his freedom—and reciprocate" (Hinman, 64)

249 With those five talents.

Exit Servant

To FLAVIUS

250 That had, give't these fellows

That had, give't: "i.e., when you have the **five talents, give** them to" (Mowat, 68); **these fellows**: "to these fellows" (Bevington)

251 To whom 'tis instant due. Ne'er speak, or think,

Instant: "now" (Mowat, 68)

252 That Timon's fortunes 'mong his friends can sink.

'Mong: "in the midst of" (Charney, 77)

FLAVIUS

253 I would I could not think it: that thought is

That . . . foe: "i.e., the naïve assumption that friends will remain true in hard times is the undoing of the bounteous impulse" (Bevington)

254 bounty's foe;

255 Being free itself, it thinks all others so.

Free: "generous" (Riverside 1,503)

Exeunt

ACT III

SCENE I. A room in Lucullus' house.

FLAMINIUS waiting. Enter a Servant to him

SERVANT

1 I have told my lord of you; he is coming down to you.

FLAMINIUS

2 I thank you, sir.

Enter LUCULLUS

SERVANT

3 Here's my lord.

LUCULLUS

4 [Aside] One of Lord Timon's men? a gift, I

5 warrant. Why, this hits right; I dreamt of a silver   **Hits right**: "fits perfectly" (Riverside 1,503)

6 basin and ewer to-night. Flaminius, honest   **Ewer**: "pitcher"; **to-night**: "last night" (Bevington)

7 Flaminius; you are very respectively welcome, sir.   **Respectively**: "particularly" (Riverside 1,504); "respectfully" (Charney, 78)

8 Fill me some wine.   **Fill me**: "i.e., pour" (Mowat, 72)

Exit Servants

9 And how does that honorable, complete, free-hearted **Complete**: "endowed with good qualities" (Riverside, 1,504); "highly accomplished" (Wright, 36)

10 gentleman of Athens, thy very bountiful good lord

11 and master?

FLAMINIUS

12 His health is well sir.

LUCULLUS

13 I am right glad that his health is well, sir: and

14 what hast thou there under thy cloak, pretty Flaminius? **Pretty**: "(vague epithet of praise)" (Charney, 79)

FLAMINIUS

15 'Faith, nothing but an empty box, sir; which, in my

16 lord's behalf, I come to entreat your honor to

17 supply; who, having great and instant occasion to **Supply**: "fill" (Riverside, 1,504); **who**: "i.e., Timon"; **instant occasion**: "pressing need" (Mowat, 72)

18 use fifty talents, hath sent to your lordship to

19 furnish him, nothing doubting your present **Nothing**: "not at all" (Bevington); **present**: "immediate" (Mowat, 74)

20 assistance therein.

LUCULLUS

21 La, la, la, la! "nothing doubting," says he? Alas,

22 good lord! a noble gentleman 'tis, if he would not **'Tis**: "he is" (Bevington)

23 keep so good a house. Many a time and often I ha' **Keep . . . house**: "offer such lavish hospitality" (Riverside, 1,504)

24 dined with him, and told him on't, and come again to **On't**: "i.e., of it" (Mowat, 74)

25 supper to him, of purpose to have him spend less,

Of purpose: "with the express purpose (of persuading him)" (Riverside, 1,504); **have him**: "i.e., persuade **him** to" (Mowat, 74)

26 and yet he would embrace no counsel, take no warning

27 by my coming. Every man has his fault, and honesty

By my: "i.e., from my" (Mowat, 74); **honesty**: "generosity" (Riverside, 1,504)

28 is his: I ha' told him on't, but I could ne'er get

29 him from't.

Re-enter Servant, with wine

SERVANT

30 Please your lordship, here is the wine.

LUCULLUS

31 Flaminius, I have noted thee always wise. Here's to thee.

FLAMINIUS

32 Your lordship speaks your pleasure.

Speaks your pleasure: "is pleased to say so" (Riverside, 1,504)

LUCULLUS

33 I have observed thee always for a towardly prompt

Towardly: "well-disposed" (Riverside, 1,504); **prompt**: "willing and ready" (Mowat, 74)

34 spirit--give thee thy due--and one that knows what

35 belongs to reason; and canst use the time well, if

Canst . . . thee well: "can make the most of an opportunity when it presents itself" (Bevington); **if the time . . . well**: "if you strike good fortune" (Charney, 79)

36 the time use thee well: good parts in thee.

Parts: "traits" (Riverside, 1,504)

To Servant

37 Get you gone, sirrah.

Sirrah: "term of address used to inferiors" (Riverside, 1,504)

Exit Servant

38 Draw nearer, honest Flaminius. Thy lord's a

39 bountiful gentleman: but thou art wise; and thou

40 knowest well enough, although thou comest to me,

41 that this is no time to lend money, especially upon

42 bare friendship, without security. Here's three

Bare "mere" (Bevington)

43 solidares for thee: good boy, wink at me, and say

Solidares: "coins (of Shakespeare's invention, from Latin *solidus*)"; **wink**: "shut your eyes" (Riverside, 1,504)

44 thou sawest me not. Fare thee well.

FLAMINIUS

45 Is't possible the world should so much differ,

So . . . lived: "i.e. be so changed in a single lifetime" (Riverside, 1,504)

46 And we alive that lived? Fly, damned baseness,

And we . . . lived: "i.e.,
the world changes so
swiftly, it is hard to
believe that the same
people are still alive"
(Charney, 80)

47 To him that worships thee!

Throwing the money back

LUCULLUS

48 Ha! now I see thou art a fool, and fit for thy master.

Exit

FLAMINIUS

49 May these add to the number that may scald thee!

These: "(the rejected
coins)" (Charney, 80);
scald: "i.e., roast in hell"
(Bevington)

50 Let molten coin be thy damnation,

Let . . . damnation:
"may you be killed (and
your soul sent to hell)
by having molten gold
poured down your throat"
(Riverside, 1,504)

51 Thou disease of a friend, and not himself!

Disease . . . himself:
"affliction to a friend but
not a friend" (Wright 38)

52 Has friendship such a faint and milky heart,

53 It turns in less than two nights? O you gods,

Turns: "sours" (Riverside,
1,504)

54 I feel master's passion! this slave,

Feel . . . passion: "i.e., feel angry on my master's behalf, share his anger and his suffering" (Bevington); **this . . . honor**: "i.e., this man who is so slavish in preserving his sense of **honor** (perhaps ironic)" (Mowat, 76); **passion**: "anger" (Wright, 38)

55 Unto his honor, has my lord's meat in him:

Unto . . . him: "i.e. much to his honor has been a guest at Timon's table. Some editors change *Unto his honor* to *Unto this hour*, after Pope; some, following F1 lineation, take the phrase back to the end of line 60 and explain *slave unto his honor* as an ironic description of Lucullus. (It would better fit Sempronius; see III. iii.32.)" (Riverside, 1,504); **meat**: "food" (Mowat, 76)

56 Why should it thrive and turn to nutriment,

57 When he is turn'd to poison?

When . . . poison: "when his behavior is so poisonous" (Bevington)

58 O, may diseases only work upon't!

Work upon 't: "thrive upon it, *my lord's meat in him*" (Bevington)

59 And, when he's sick to death, let not that part of nature

Nature: "i.e., Lucullus' body" (Wright 38)

60 Which my lord paid for, be of any power

61 To expel sickness, but prolong his hour!

His hour: "i.e. his time of suffering before death" (Riverside, 1,504)

Exit

SCENE II. A public place.

Enter LUCILIUS, with three Strangers

Strangers: "foreigners, non-Athenians" (Charney, 81)

LUCILIUS

1 Who, the Lord Timon? he is my very good friend, and

2 an honorable gentleman.

FIRST STRANGER

3 We know him for no less, though we are but strangers

For no less: "to be no less than you say" (Bevington)

4 to him. But I can tell you one thing, my lord, and

5 which I hear from common rumors: now Lord Timon's

Which: "i.e., one **which**" (Mowat, 76)

6 happy hours are done and past, and his estate

Happy: "fortunate" (Mowat, 76)

7 shrinks from him.

LUCILIUS

8 Fie, no, do not believe it; he cannot want for money.

Want for: "lack" (Mowat, 76)

SECOND STRANGER

9 But believe you this, my lord, that, not long ago,

10 one of his men was with the Lord Lucullus to borrow

11 so many talents, nay, urged extremely for't and

So many talents: "(an indefinite number probably intended to be replaced, in revision, by a definite number)" (Charney, 81); **urged extremely**: "begged insistently" (Bevington)

12 showed what necessity belonged to 't, and yet was denied.

What . . . to 't: "how necessary it was" (Bevington)

LUCILIUS

13 How!

How: "i.e., what did you say" (Mowat, 78)

SECOND STRANGER

14 I tell you, denied, my lord.

LUCILIUS

15 What a strange case was that! now, before the gods,

16 I am ashamed on't. Denied that honorable man!

17 there was very little honor showed in't. For my own

18 part, I must needs confess, I have received some

19 small kindnesses from him, as money, plate, jewels

Plate: "silver or gold utensils or ornaments" (Mowat, 78)

20 and such-like trifles, nothing comparing to his;

His: "i.e. what Lucullus has received" (Riverside, 1,504)

21 yet, had he mistook him and sent to me, I should

Mistook . . . me: "i.e. by mistake sent his messenger to me, who owed him less (instead of to Lucullus)" (Riverside, 1,504)

22 ne'er have denied his occasion so many talents.

Denied . . . talents: "i.e., **denied** him **fifty talents** in his need" (Mowat, 78); **occasion**: "need" (Charney, 81)

Enter SERVILIUS

SERVILIUS

23 See, by good hap, yonder's my lord;

Hap: "luck" (Riverside, 1,504); **my lord**: "i.e., Lucius" (Mowat, 78)

24 I have sweat to see his honor. My honored lord--

Sweat: "i.e., sweated, exerted myself strongly" (Mowat, 78)

To LUCIUS

LUCILIUS

25 Servilius! you are kindly met, sir. Fare thee well:

26 commend me to thy honorable virtuous lord, my very

27 exquisite friend.

Exquisite: "excellent" (Mowat, 78); "sought after" (Bevington)

SERVILIUS

28 May it please your honor, my lord hath sent--

LUCILIUS

29 Ha! what has he sent? I am so much endeared to

Endeared: "obliged" (Mowat, 78)

30 that lord; he's ever sending: how shall I thank

31 him, thinkest thou? And what has he sent now?

SERVILIUS

32 H'as only sent his present occasion now, my lord;

H'as: "he has" (Riverside, 1,504); **occasion**: "need" (Mowat, 78)

33 requesting your lordship to supply his instant use

Supply . . . use: "i.e., provide him immediately" (Mowat, 78)

Donald J. Richardson

34 with so many talents.

LUCILIUS

35 I know his lordship is but merry with me;

36 He cannot want fifty-five hundred talents.

Want: "(1) be without, lack (2) need, desire" 82); **fifty-five . . . talents**: "160 *tons* of silver" (Asimov, 139)

SERVILIUS

37 But in the mean time he wants less, my lord.

Wants: "wordplay on **want** as 'desire, wish'" (Mowat, 78)

38 If his occasion were not virtuous,

Were not virtuous: "i.e., did not arise from the practice of virtue, i.e., generosity" (Mowat, 78); **virtuous**: "honorable" (Wright, 40)

39 I should not urge it half so faithfully.

LUCILIUS

40 Dost thou speak seriously, Servilius?

SERVILIUS

41 Upon my soul,'tis true, sir.

LUCILIUS

42 What a wicked beast was I to disfurnish myself

Disfurnish . . . time: "i.e., deprive **myself** (of what is needed) just before such a **good** opportunity" (Mowat, 80)

43 against such a good time, when I might ha' shown

Against: "on the eve of" (Williams, 39); **against . . . time**: "for dealing with such an opportunity" (Hinman, 69)

44 myself honorable! how unluckily it happened, that I

That I . . . honor: "i.e., that I just yesterday laid out a sum of money in a small investment and thus made it impossible now to acquire a great honor by helping Timon" (Bevington)

45 should purchase the day before for a little part,

Purchase: "strive" (Mowat, 80); **for . . . honor**: "what brings me little honor, and (thus) lose a chance to win a great deal of honor" (Riverside, 1,505)

46 and undo a great deal of honor! Servilius, now,

Undo . . . honor: "i.e., lose the anticipated honor of lending to Timon" (Charney, 82)

47 before the gods, I am not able to do (the more

48 beast, I say!)--I was sending to use Lord Timon

Use: "borrow from" (Riverside, 1,505)

49 myself, these gentlemen can witness! but I would

I would not . . . I had done 't: "i.e., I wish . . . that **I had not done** it" (Mowat, 80

50 not, for the wealth of Athens, I had done't now.

51 Commend me bountifully to his good lordship; and I

52 hope his honor will conceive the fairest of me,

Conceive . . . me: "regard me in the most favorable light" (Riverside, 1,505)

53 because I have no power to be kind: and tell him

Because: "i.e., even though" (Bevington)

54 this from me, I count it one of my greatest

55 afflictions, say, that I cannot pleasure such an

Pleasure: "satisfy, please" (Bevington)

56 honorable gentleman. Good Servilius, will you

57 befriend me so far, as to use mine own words to him?

SERVILIUS

58 Yes, sir, I shall.

LUCILIUS

59 I'll look you out a good turn, Servilius.

I'll . . . turn: "i.e., **I'll** be on the lookout for something I can do for **you**" (Mowat, 80)

Exit SERVILIUS

60 True as you said, Timon is shrunk indeed;

Shrunk: "brought low" (Bevington)

61 And he that's once denied will hardly speed.

Speed: "prosper" (Riverside, 1,505)

Exit

FIRST STRANGER

62 Do you observe this, Hostilius?

SECOND STRANGER

63 Ay, too well.

FIRST STRANGER

64 Why, this is the world's soul; and just of the

World's soul: "principle that animates the world"; **just . . . piece**: "i.e., exactly the **same**" (Mowat, 80)

65 same piece

Piece: "sort, kind" (Charney, 83)

66 Is every flatterer's sport. Who can call him

Sport: "mockery. Many editors adopt Theobald's reading *spirit*." (Riverside, 1,505)

67 His friend that dips in the same dish? for, in

Dips . . . dish: "Compare Matthew 26.23: 'He that dippeth his hand with me in **the dish**, he shall betray me.'" (Mowat, 80)

68 My knowing, Timon has been this lord's father,

Father: "i.e., patron" (Bevington); "sponsor, protector" (Hinman, 70)

69 And kept his credit with his purse,

Kept his credit: "maintained Lucius' credit" (Riverside, 1,505); **with his**: "i.e., **with** Timon's own" (Mowat, 80)

70 Supported his estate; nay, Timon's money

71 Has paid his men their wages: he ne'er drinks,

72 But Timon's silver treads upon his lip;

Treads: "rests its weight" (Riverside, 1,505)

73 And yet--O, see the monstrousness of man

74 When he looks out in an ungrateful shape!—

Looks out: "appears" (Mowat, 82); **shape**: "form" (Charney, 83)

75 He does deny him, in respect of his,

He: "i.e., Lucius" (Mowat, 82); **in . . . his**: "in proportion to his resources" (Riverside, 1,505)

76 What charitable men afford to beggars.

THIRD STRANGER

77 Religion groans at it.

Religion: "proper feeling" (Williams, 40)

FIRST STRANGER

78 For mine own part,

79 I never tasted Timon in my life,

Tasted Timon: "i.e. sampled his generosity" (Riverside, 1,505)

80 Nor came any of his bounties over me,

Came . . . me: "was I the recipient of any of his generosity" (Bevington)

81 To mark me for his friend; yet, I protest,

Protest: "avow" (Riverside, 1,505)

82 For his right noble mind, illustrious virtue

For: "because of" (Mowat, 82); **right**: "very" (Charney, 84)

83 And honorable carriage,

Carriage: "conduct" (Riverside, 1,505)

84 Had his necessity made use of me,

Made use of me: "i.e., sought my aid" (Bevington)

85 I would have put my wealth into donation,

Put . . . donation: "regarded my wealth as a gift (from Timon)" (Riverside, 1,505)

86 And the best half should have return'd to him,

Best half: "greater part"; **return'd**: "i.e., gone back as if to its previous owner" (Mowat, 82)

87 So much I love his heart: but, I perceive,

88 Men must learn now with pity to dispense;

89 For policy sits above conscience.

Policy: "cunning dissimulation" (Mowat, 82)

Exeunt

SCENE III. A room in Sempronius' house.

Enter SEMPRONIUS, and a Servant of TIMON's

SEMPRONIUS

1 Must he needs trouble me in 't--hum!--'bove

Must . . . me: "**in 't**: "i.e., with it" (Mowat, 82)

2 all others?

3 He might have tried Lord Lucius or Lucullus;

4 And now Ventidius is wealthy too,

5 Whom he redeem'd from prison: all these

6 Owe their estates unto him.

SERVANT

7 My lord,

8 They have all been touch'd and found base metal, for

Touch'd: "tested (by being rubbed on a touchstone, to see whether they are gold or base metal)" (Riverside, 1,505)

9 They have all denied him.

Denied: "refused" (Hinman, 71)

SEMPRONIUS

10 How! have they denied him?

11 Has Ventidius and Lucullus denied him?

Has: "i.e., have" (Mowat, 82)

12 And does he send to me? Three? hum!

Three: "(Lucius as well as Ventidius and Lucullus)" (Hinman, 71)

13 It shows but little love or judgment in him:

14 Must I be his last refuge! His friends, like

His friends . . . over: "Proverbial: '**Physicians** enriched **give over** their patients.'"; **give over**: "declare incurable" (Mowat, 84)

15 physicians,

16 Thrive, give him over: must I take the cure upon me?

Thrive . . . over: "i.e. thrive on his money but declare his case hopeless and make no effort to help him" (Riverside, 1,505)

17 Has much disgraced me in't; I'm angry at him,

Has: "i.e., he **has**" (Mowat, 84)

18 That might have known my place: I see no sense for't,

That . . . place: "i.e., who should have granted me precedence among his friends"; **sense**: "reason" (Mowat, 84); **I . . . first**: "I see no reason why, in his need, he did not apply to me first." (Riverside, 1,505)

19 But his occasions might have woo'd me first;

His occasions: "i.e., he, in his need" (Mowat, 84)

20 For, in my conscience, I was the first man

In my conscience: "truly" (Mowat, 84); "to my knowledge" (Hinman, 71)

21 That e'er received gift from him:

22 And does he think so backwardly of me now,

Think . . . me: "i.e. think me so slow and reluctant" (Riverside, 1,505)

23 That I'll requite it last? No:

Requite: "repay" (Wright, 43)

24 So it may prove an argument of laughter

Argument of: "matter for" (Riverside, 1,505); "theme" (Wright, 43)

25 To the rest, and 'mongst lords I be thought a fool.

26 I'ld rather than the worth of thrice the sum,

27 Had sent to me first, but for my mind's sake;

Had: "i.e., he **had**: (Mowat, 84); **but . . . sake**: "if only because of my good will toward him" (Riverside, 1,505)

28 I'd such a courage to do him good. But now return,

Courage: "heart, i.e. desire" (Riverside, 1,505); "determination" (Wright, 43); "inclination" (Hinman, 72)

29 And with their faint reply this answer join;

Faint: "timid" (Williams, 42)

30 Who bates mine honor shall not know my coin.

Bates: "undervalues (?) or diminishes (?)" (Riverside, 1,505)

Exit

SERVANT

31 Excellent! Your lordship's a goodly villain. The

Goodly: "splendid, excellent" (Mowat, 84); "(Said ironically.)" (Bevington)

32 devil knew not what he did when he made man

33 politic; he cross'd himself by 't: and I cannot

Politic: "crafty"(Riverside, 1,505); **cross'd himself**: "(1) thwarted himself; (2) made himself seem guiltless in comparison" (Wright, 43)

34 think but, in the end, the villainies of man will

35 set him clear. How fairly this lord strives to

Set him clear: "(1) make him appear innocent; (2) cancel his debt of evil" (Wright, 43); **how fairly**: "with what an appearance of virtue" (Riverside, 1,505)

36 appear foul! takes virtuous copies to be wicked,

Foul: "ugly" (Charney, 85); **takes . . . wicked**: "for his wicked ends models himself on the virtuous" (Riverside, 1,505)

37 like those that under hot ardent zeal would set

Those . . . fire: "i.e. those who cause great disturbances in the state for religious ends" (Riverside, 1,506)

38 whole realms on fire: Of such a nature is his

39 politic love.

40 This was my lord's best hope; now all are fled,

41 Save only the gods: now his friends are dead,

Now: "now that" (Bevington)

42 Doors, that were ne'er acquainted with their wards

Wards: "locks (literally, the ridges projecting from the inside plate of a lock)" (Mowat, 84)

43 Many a bounteous year must be employ'd

Many: "for many" (Bevington)

44 Now to guard sure their master.

Guard . . . master: "i.e. from arrest for debt" (Riverside, 1,506); **sure**: "securely" (Charney, 86)

45 And this is all a liberal course allows;

Liberal: "generous" (Riverside, 1,506)

46 Who cannot keep his wealth must keep his house.

Keep . . . keep: "i.e., stay in **his house** so as not to be arrested for debt" (Mowat, 84)

Exit

SCENE IV. The same. A hall in Timon's house.

Enter two Servants of Varro, and the Servant of LUCIUS, meeting TITUS, HORTENSIUS, and other Servants of TIMON's creditors, waiting his coming out

VARRO'S FIRST SERVANT

1 Well met; good morrow, Titus and Hortensius.

Morrow: "morning" (Mowat, 86)

TITUS

2 The like to you kind Varro.

Like: "same" (Mowat, 86)

HORTENSIUS

3 Lucius!

4 What, do we meet together?

What: "an interjection introducing a question" (Mowat, 86)

LUCILIUS' SERVANT

5 Ay, and I think

6 One business does command us all; for mine is money.

TITUS

7 So is theirs and ours.

Enter PHILOTUS

LUCILIUS' SERVANT

8 And Sir Philotus too!

Sir: "a facetious dignity" (Wright, 44)

PHILOTUS

9 Good day at once.

At once: "to you all" (Riverside, 1,506)

LUCILIUS' SERVANT

10 Welcome, good brother.

11 What do you think the hour?

PHILOTUS

12 Laboring for nine.

Laboring for: "moving toward" (Bevington)

109

LUCILIUS' SERVANT

13 So much?

Much: "i.e., late" (Bevington)

PHILOTUS

14 Is not my lord seen yet?

LUCILIUS' SERVANT

15 Not yet.

PHILOTUS

16 I wonder on't; he was wont to shine at seven.

Was ... shine: "used to be up" (Bevington)

LUCILIUS'S SERVANT

17 Ay, but the days are wax'd shorter with him:

Wax'd: "become" (Riverside, 1,506)

18 You must consider that a prodigal course

Prodigal: "extravagant" (Wright, 45)

19 Is like the sun's; but not, like his, recoverable.

Like the sun's: "i.e., it blazes gloriously but later declines" (Wright, 45); **recoverable**: "(1) capable of being retraced; (2) capable of being recovered or regained" (Mowat, 86)

20 I fear 'tis deepest winter in Lord Timon's purse;

21 That is one may reach deep enough, and yet

Reach deep enough: "(as do animals digging deep in the snow for food)" (Hinman, 74)

22 Find little.

PHILOTUS

23 I am of your fear for that.

Am of: "share" (Bevington)

TITUS

24 I'll show you how to observe a strange event.

Observe: "i.e., analyze" (Bevington)

25 Your lord sends now for money.

Money: "i.e. the loan which Timon cannot repay, since he spent it on jewels for Hortensius' master" (Riverside, 1,506)

HORTENSIUS

26 Most true, he does.

TITUS

27 And he wears jewels now of Timon's gift,

28 For which I wait for money.

HORTENSIUS

29 It is against my heart.

Heart: "wish, feeling" (Bevington)

LUCILIUS' SERVANT

30 Mark, how strange it shows,

Mark: "notice, consider" (Mowat, 88); **shows**: "appears" (Williams, 44)

31 Timon in this should pay more than he owes:

Should . . . owes: "i.e., he has given the gifts, and now he is also asked for the money for them" (Charney, 87)

32 And e'en as if your lord should wear rich jewels,

E'en . . . for 'em: "i.e., it's just as though your master should both wear the jewels Timon gave him and simultaneously demand the money that paid for those jewels" (Bevington)

33 And send for money for 'em.

HORTENSIUS

34 I'm weary of this charge, the gods can witness:

Charge: "commission" (Riverside, 1,506); "task" (Mowat, 88)

35 I know my lord hath spent of Timon's wealth,   **Spent**: "made use" (Bevington)

36 And now ingratitude makes it worse than stealth.   **Stealth**: "stealing" (Riverside, 1,506)

VARRO'S FIRST SERVANT

37 Yes, mine's three thousand crowns: what's yours?

LUCILIUS' SERVANT

38 Five thousand mine.

VARRO'S FIRST SERVANT

39 'Tis much deep: and it should seem by the sun,   **Much**: "very" (Mowat, 88)

40 Your master's confidence was above mine;   **Above mine**: "i.e. greater than my master's confidence" (Riverside, 1,506); **confidence**: "impudent presumption" (Wright, 45); "trust" (Charney, 88)

41 Else, surely, his had equall'd.   **His had equall'd**: "i.e. my master's loan would have equalled your master's" (Riverside, 1,506)

Enter FLAMINIUS.

TITUS

42 One of Lord Timon's men.

LUCILIUS' SERVANT

43 Flaminius! Sir, a word: pray,

44 is my lord ready to come forth?

FLAMINIUS

45 No, indeed, he is not.

TITUS

46 We attend his lordship; pray, signify so much.

Attend: "wait for" (Mowat, 88)

FLAMINIUS

47 I need not tell him that; he knows you are too diligent.

Diligent: "attentive" (Mowat, 88)

Exit

Enter FLAVIUS in a cloak, muffled

Muffled: "wrapped up, especially about the face" (Charney, 88)

LUCILIUS' SERVANT

48 Ha! is not that his steward muffled so?

49 He goes away in a cloud: call him, call him.

In a cloud: "(1) as if covered by a cloud; (2) in a state of gloom" (Riverside, 1,506)

TITUS

50 Do you hear, sir?

VARRO'S SECOND SERVANT

51 By your leave, sir--

FLAVIUS

52 What do ye ask of me, my friend?

TITUS

53 We wait for certain money here, sir.

Certain: "sure to come, dependable" (Mowat, 90)

FLAVIUS

54 Ay,

55 If money were as certain as your waiting,

56 'Twere sure enough.

57 Why then preferr'd you not your sums and bills,

Preferr'd: "proffered, presented" (Riverside, 1,506)

58 When your false masters eat of my lord's meat?

Eat: "ate (pronounced *et*)" (Riverside, 1,506); **meat**: "food" (Mowat, 90)

59 Then they could smile and fawn upon his debts

Fawn upon: "seek favor by servility (used especially of dogs)" (Charney, 89)

60 And take down th' int'rest into their

Th' int'rest: "i.e., the food and drink they consumed as though it were interest on the loans" (Bevington)

61 gluttonous maws.

62 You do yourselves but wrong to stir me up;

Do yourselves . . . wrong: "only waste your time" (Wright, 46)

63 Let me pass quietly:

64 Believe 't, my lord and I have made an end;

Made an end: "parted company" (Riverside, 1,506)

65 I have no more to reckon, he to spend.

Reckon: "keep account of" (Bevington)

LUCILIUS' SERVANT

66 Ay, but this answer will not serve.

Will not serve: "does not satisfy" (Mowat, 90)

FLAVIUS

67 If 'twill not serve,'tis not so base as you;

68 For you serve knaves.

You serve: "i.e., **you** act as servants to" (Mowat, 90)

Exit

VARRO'S FIRST SERVANT

69 How! what does his cashier'd worship mutter?

Cashier'd: "dismissed" (Riverside, 1,506)

VARRO'S SECOND SERVANT

70 No matter what; he's poor, and that's revenge

71 enough. Who can speak broader than he that has | **Broader**: "more freely"
no | (Riverside, 1,506)

72 house to put his head in? such may rail against | **Such . . . buildings**: "i.e., a man who is houseless and out of service, like Flavius, has nothing to lose and can inveigh against injustice and inequality" (Bevington)

73 great buildings.

Enter SERVILIUS

TITUS

74 O, here's Servilius; now we shall know some answer.

SERVILIUS

75 If I might beseech you, gentlemen, to repair some | **Repair**: "come back" (Riverside, 1,507)

76 other hour, I should derive much from't; for, | **Derive**: "gain" (Mowat, 90)

77 take't of my soul, my lord leans wondrously to | **Take't . . . soul**: "i.e., believe I speak sincerely" (Bevington)

78 discontent: his comfortable temper has forsook him; | **Comfortable**: "cheerful" (Riverside, 1,507)

79 he's much out of health, and keeps his chamber. | **Keeps**: "stays in" (Bevington)

LUCILIUS' SERVANT

80 Many do keep their chambers are not sick: | **Chambers are**: "i.e., **chambers** who **are**" (Mowat, 92)

81 And, if it be so far beyond his health, | **If . . . health**: "if he has indeed passed beyond good health" (Riverside, 1,507)

82 Methinks he should the sooner pay his debts,

83 And make a clear way to the gods.

Make a clear . . . gods: "clear himself of guilt in preparation for Heaven" (Wright, 47)

SERVILIUS

84 Good gods!

TITUS

85 We cannot take this for answer, sir.

FLAMINIUS

86 [Within] Servilius, help! My lord! my lord!

Within: "i.e., from offstage" (Mowat, 92)

Enter TIMON, in a rage, FLAMINIUS following

TIMON

87 What, are my doors opposed against my passage?

88 Have I been ever free, and must my house

Free: "with wordplay on the meaning 'generous'" (Mowat, 92)

89 Be my retentive enemy, my jail?

Retentive: "confining (with possible wordplay on the meaning 'stingy')" (Mowat, 92)

90 The place which I have feasted, does it now,

Feasted: "made festive (?) or feasted in (?)" (Riverside, 1,507)

91 Like all mankind, show me an iron heart?

LUCILIUS' SERVANT

92 Put in now, Titus.

Put in: "i.e., present (your claim)" (Mowat, 92)

TITUS

93 My lord, here is my bill.

LUCILIUS' SERVANT

94 Here's mine.

HORTENSIUS

95 And mine, my lord.

BOTH VARRO'S SERVANTS

96 And ours, my lord.

PHILOTUS

97 All our bills.

TIMON

98 Knock me down with 'em: cleave me to the girdle.

Knock . . . girdle: "Timon quibbles on *bills* in the sense 'watchmen's pikes.'" (Riverside, 1,507); **girdle**: "belt" (Mowat, 92); **cleave me**: "Timon speaks as though the bills were halberd-like weapons of the same name." (Wright, 48)

LUCILIUS' SERVANT

99 Alas, my lord--

TIMON

100 Cut my heart in sums.

Sums: "i.e. sufficient pieces to make up the sums demanded" (Riverside, 1,507)

TITUS

101 Mine, fifty talents.

TIMON

102 Tell out my blood.

Tell out: "count out drop by drop" (Riverside, 1,507)

LUCILIUS' SERVANT

103 Five thousand crowns, my lord.

TIMON

104 Five thousand drops pays that.

105 What yours?--and yours?

VARRO'S FIRST SERVANT

106 My lord--

VARRO'S SECOND SERVANT

107 My lord--

TIMON

108 Tear me, take me, and the gods fall upon you!   **Fall upon**: "i.e., rush to attack" (Mowat, 94)

Exit

HORTENSIUS

109 'Faith, I perceive our masters may throw their caps   **Throw . . . / at**: "give up all hope of" (Riverside, 1,507)

110 at their money: these debts may well be called

111 desperate ones, for a madman owes 'em.   **Desperate**: "beyond recovery (with wordplay on the meaning 'infuriated from despair,' with reference to Timon)" (Mowat, 94)

Exeunt

Re-enter TIMON and FLAVIUS

TIMON

112 They have e'en put my breath from me, the slaves.   **E'en . . . me**: "i.e., made me speechless with rage" (Wright, 48)

113 Creditors? devils!

FLAVIUS

114 My dear lord--

TIMON

115 What if it should be so?

What . . . so: "i.e. suppose I do it. (Timon has just conceived the idea of the banquet of III.vi.)" (Riverside, 1,507)

FLAVIUS

116 My lord--

TIMON

117 I'll have it so. My steward!

FLAVIUS

118 Here, my lord.

TIMON

119 So fitly? Go, bid all my friends again,

Fitly: "readily" (Mowat, 94); **bid**: "invite" (Charney, 91)

120 Lucius, Lucullus, and Sempronius:

121 All, sirrah, all:

122 I'll once more feast the rascals.

FLAVIUS

123 O my lord,

124 You only speak from your distracted soul;

125 There is not so much left, to furnish out

To: "as to" (Riverside, 1,507); **furnish out**: "provide enough for" (Mowat, 94)

126 A moderate table.

TIMON

127 Be't not in thy care; go,

Be . . . care: "that's not your responsibility" (Riverside, 1,507)

128 I charge thee, invite them all: let in the tide

129 Of knaves once more; my cook and I'll provide.

Exeunt

SCENE V. The same. The senate-house. The Senate sitting.

FIRST SENATOR

1 My lord, you have my voice to 't; the fault's

Voice to 't: "vote in favor of it" (Riverside, 1,507); **fault's**: "offense is" (Mowat, 96)

2 Bloody; 'tis necessary he should die:

3 Nothing emboldens sin so much as mercy

Nothing . . . mercy: "Proverbial: 'Pardon makes offenders.'" (Mowat, 96).

SECOND SENATOR

4 Most true; the law shall bruise 'em.

Bruise: "crush, smash" (Mowat, 96); **'em**: "i.e. sinners" (Riverside, 1,507)

Enter ALCIBIADES, with Attendants

ALCIBIADES

5 Honor, health, and compassion to the senate!

Compassion to the senate: "i.e., may the Senate have compassion" (Bevington)

FIRST SENATOR

6 Now, captain?

ALCIBIADES

7 I am an humble suitor to your virtues;

8 For pity is the virtue of the law,

Virtue: "excellence, merit" (Riverside, 1,507)

9 And none but tyrants use it cruelly.

It: "i.e., **the law**" (Mowat, 96)

10 It pleases time and fortune to lie heavy

Lie . . . / Upon: "oppress" (Bevington)

11 Upon a friend of mine, who, in hot blood,

12 Hath stepp'd into the law, which is past depth

Stepp'd into: "incurred the penalties of" (Bevington); **past depth / To**: "over the head of" (Riverside, 1,507); "bottomless" (Wright, 50)

13 To those that, without heed, do plunge into 't.

14 He is a man, setting his fate aside,

Setting . . . aside: "discounting" (Wright, 50); **his fate**: "i.e. the deed he was fated to do. Some editors read *his* (or *this*) *fault*, after Warburton and Pope." (Riverside, 1,507)

15 Of comely virtues:

16 Nor did he soil the fact with cowardice--

Soil the fact: "sully the deed" (Charney, 92)

17 An honor in him which buys out his fault--

Buys out: "redeems" (Riverside, 1,507); **fault**: "culpability" (Mowat, 96)

18 But with a noble fury and fair spirit,

Fair: "honorable" (Wright, 50)

19 Seeing his reputation touch'd to death,

Touch'd to death: "threatened with fatal injury" (Riverside, 1,507)

20 He did oppose his foe:

21 And with such sober and unnoted passion

Sober: "moderate" (Wright, 50); **unnoted**: "i.e. so well under control as to be without visible symptoms" (Riverside, 1,507)

22 He did behoove his anger, ere 'twas spent,

Behoove: "make seemly. Most editors adopt Rowe's emendation, *behave*, i.e. manage, regulate." (Riverside, 1,507)

23 As if he had but proved an argument.

But . . . argument: "only been testing a philosophical proposition" (Bevington)

FIRST SENATOR

24 You undergo too strict a paradox,

Undergo . . . paradox: "maintain an absolute absurdity" (Wright, 50)

25 Striving to make an ugly deed look fair:

26 Your words have took such pains as if they labor'd

Took: "i.e., taken" (Mowat, 96)

27 To bring manslaughter into form and set quarrelling

Bring into form: "make . . . a formal procedure"; **set . . . head**: "treat quarreling as a subdivision of" (Riverside, 1,508)

28 Upon the head of valor; which indeed

Upon the head of: "under the heading of" (Wright, 50); **which**: "i.e. quarrelling" (Riverside, 1,508)

29 Is valor misbegot and came into the world

Misbegot: "misbegotten, illegitimately fathered" (Mowat, 98)

30 When sects and factions were newly born:

31 He's truly valiant that can wisely suffer

32 The worst that man can breathe, and make his wrongs

Breathe: "speak"; **his wrongs**: "i.e., the **wrongs** he endures" (Mowat, 98)

33 His outsides, to wear them like his raiment,

His outsides: "merely external circumstance"; **raiment**: "clothing" (Bevington)

34 carelessly,

Carelessly: "unconcernedly" (Riverside, 1,508)

35 And ne'er prefer his injuries to his heart,

Prefer: "present" (Riverside, 1,508)

36 To bring it into danger.

37 If wrongs be evils and enforce us kill,

If . . . ill: "(some senators are less lucid then sententious)" (Hinman, 79); **us kill**: "i.e., **us** to kill" (Mowat, 98)

38 What folly 'tis to hazard life for ill!

Hazard . . . ill: "risk one's life when the only profit can be another evil" (Wright, 51); **for ill**: "in a bad cause" (Bevington)

ALCIBIADES

39 My lord--

FIRST SENATOR

40 You cannot make gross sins look clear:

Gross: "glaring" (Wright, 51); **clear**: "innocent" (Mowat, 98)

41 To revenge is no valor, but to bear.

To revenge . . . bear: "proverbially, 'The noblest vengeance is to forgive.'" (Wright, 51); **bear**: "endure" (Mowat, 98)

ALCIBIADES

42 My lords, then, under favor, pardon me,

Under favor: "by your leave" (Riverside, 1,508)

43 If I speak like a captain.

44 Why do fond men expose themselves to battle,

Fond: "foolish" (Riverside, 1,508)

45 And not endure all threats? sleep upon't,

Sleep: "i.e., why do they not sleep" (Bevington)

46 And let the foes quietly cut their throats,

47 Without repugnancy? If there be

Repugnancy: "fighting back" (Riverside, 1,508)

48 Such valor in the bearing, what make we

What . . . / Abroad: "i.e., why do we go on foreign military expeditions in defense of our state?" (Mowat, 98); **make**: "do" (Riverside, 1,508)

49 Abroad? why then, women are more valiant

Abroad: "away from home" (Riverside, 1,508)

50 That stay at home, if bearing carry it,

Bearing: "putting up with insults (with a pun on 'childbearing' and perhaps on 'supporting the man in sexual intercourse')" (Bevington); **carry it**: "gains the advantage; wins the day" (Mowat, 98)

51 And the ass more captain than the lion, the fellow

More captain than: "superior to"; **fellow**: "Many editors adopt Theobald's conjecture *felon*." (Riverside, 1,508)

52 Loaden with irons wiser than the judge,

Loaden with irons: "laden with iron shackles" (Mowat, 98)

53 If wisdom be in suffering. O my lords,

54 As you are great, be pitifully good:

Pitifully good: "good in showing pity" (Wright, 51)

55 Who cannot condemn rashness in cold blood?

56 To kill, I grant, is sin's extremest gust;

Sin's extremest gust: "'the utmost degree of appetite for sin' (Johnson) (?) or sin's utmost violence (metaphor from wind) (?)" (Riverside, 1,508); "(*Gust* means outburst, indulgence.)" (Bevington)

57 But, in defense, by mercy, 'tis most just.

By mercy: "mercifully interpreted" (Riverside, 1,508)

58 To be in anger is impiety;

59 But who is man that is not angry?

Not: "i.e. never" (Riverside, 1,508)

60 Weigh but the crime with this.

SECOND SENATOR

61 You breathe in vain.

Breathe in vain: "waste your breath" (Williams, 49)

ALCIBIADES

62 In vain! his service done

63 At Lacedaemon and Byzantium

64 Were a sufficient briber for his life.

Briber: "advocate" (Williams, 50)

FIRST SENATOR

65 What's that?

ALCIBIADES

66 I say, my lords, h'as done fair service,

Say: "let us say, let us admit" (Charney, 94); **h'as done**: "i.e., he **has done**"; **fair**: "fine" (Mowat, 100)

67 And slain in fight many of your enemies:

68 How full of valor did he bear himself

69 In the last conflict, and made plenteous wounds!

SECOND SENATOR

70 He has made too much plenty with 'em;

He . . . 'em: "he has used them as an excuse for too much riotous living (?)" (Riverside, 1,508)

71 He's a sworn rioter: he has a sin that often

Sworn rioter: "inveterate reveler"; **sin**: "i.e. drunkenness" (Riverside, 1,508)

72 Drowns him, and takes his valor prisoner:

73 If there were no foes, that were enough

If: "even if" (Riverside, 1,508); **foes**: "accusers" (Bevington); **that were enough**: "i.e., his drinking would be **enough**" (Mowat, 100)

74 To overcome him: in that beastly fury

75 He has been known to commit outrages,

76 And cherish factions: 'tis inferr'd to us,

Cherish factions: "support subversive elements"; **inferr'd**: "alleged" (Riverside, 1,508)

77 His days are foul and his drink dangerous.

FIRST SENATOR

78 He dies.

ALCIBIADES

79 Hard fate! he might have died in war.

80 My lords, if not for any parts in him--

Parts: "good qualities" (Riverside, 1,508)

81 Though his right arm might purchase his own time

Purchase: "beginning a financial figure that continues throughout the speech"; **his own time**: "the right to his natural term of life" (Riverside, 1,508)

82 And be in debt to none--yet, more to move you,

83 Take my deserts to his, and join 'em both:

To his: "i.e., in addition **to his**" (Mowat, 100)

84 And, for I know your reverend ages love

For: "because" (Riverside, 1,508)

85 Security, I'll pawn my victories, all

Security: "(1) safety; (2) collateral for a loan" (Riverside, 1,508); "Wordplay on financial terms continues with **pawn, good returns,** and **owes**.)" (Mowat, 100)

86 My honors to you, upon his good returns.

Upon: "as a guarantee of"; **good returns**: "(1) high profit; (2) good behavior" (Riverside, 1,508)

87 If by this crime he owes the law his life,

88 Why, let the war receive 't in valiant gore

Let . . . gore: "i.e., let him pay his debt by bleeding as a soldier" (Bevington)

89 For law is strict, and war is nothing more.

Law . . . more: "i.e., war is as merciless as the law" (Wright, 52)

FIRST SENATOR

90 We are for law: he dies; urge it no more,

91 On height of our displeasure: friend or brother,

On . . . our: "on pain of our highest" (Riverside, 1,508)

92 He forfeits his own blood that spills another.

Spills: "destroys" (Williams, 50); **another**: "another's" (Riverside, 1,508)

ALCIBIADES

93 Must it be so? it must not be. My lords,

94 I do beseech you, know me.

SECOND SENATOR

95 How!

How: "i.e., what do you mean" (Mowat, 102)

ALCIBIADES

96 Call me to your remembrances.

THIRD SENATOR

97 What!

ALCIBIADES

98 I cannot think but your age has forgot me;

Your age: "the forgetfulness of your old age" (Wright, 53)

99 It could not else be, I should prove so base,

Else be: "otherwise be (that)"; **prove**: "i.e., be considered" (Bevington)

100 To sue, and be denied such common grace:

Sue: "petition" (Mowat, 102); **common grace**: "i.e. a favor you might be expected to grant any man" (Riverside, 1,508)

101 My wounds ache at you.

FIRST SENATOR

102 Do you dare our anger?

103 'Tis in few words, but spacious in effect;

Spacious in effect: "of great import (with quibble on the spacious world to which Alcibiades is banished)" (Bevington)

104 We banish thee for ever.

ALCIBIADES

105 Banish me!

106 Banish your dotage; banish usury,

107 That makes the senate ugly.

FIRST SENATOR

108 If, after two days' shine, Athens contain thee,

Two days' shine: "i.e., two days" (Mowat, 102)

109 Attend our weightier judgment. And, not to swell

Attend . . . judgment: "expect our severer sentence" (Riverside, 1,508); **not to . . . spirit**: "lest our anger grow" (Wright, 53)

110 our spirit,

Spirit: "anger" (Riverside, 1,508)

111 He shall be executed presently.

Presently: "immediately" (Riverside, 1,508)

Exeunt Senators

ALCIBIADES

112 Now the gods keep you old enough; that you may live

113 Only in bone, that none may look on you!

Only in bone: "i.e. as mere skeletons" (Riverside, 1,508)

114 I'm worse than mad: I have kept back their foes,

115 While they have told their money and let out

Told: "counted" (Riverside, 1,508); **let out**: "loaned" (Mowat, 102)

116 Their coin upon large interest, I myself

117 Rich only in large hurts. All those for this?

Hurts: "injuries" (Bevington)

118 Is this the balsom that the usuring senate

Balsom: "balsam, healing ointment" (Riverside, 1,508)

119 Pours into captains' wounds? Banishment!

120 It comes not ill; I hate not to be banish'd;

It comes not ill: "that's not so bad" (Wright, 53)

121 It is a cause worthy my spleen and fury,

Worthy: "worthy of" (Bevington) **spleen**: "malice, passionate hatred" (Charney, 96)

122 That I may strike at Athens. I'll cheer up

123 My discontented troops, and lay for hearts.

Lay for hearts: "with their support (literally, ambush affections)" (Riverside, 1,509)

124 'Tis honor with most lands to be at odds;

'Tis honor . . . odds: "it is honorable in most countries to be warlike" (Wright, 53)

125 Soldiers should brook as little wrongs as gods.

Brook . . . gods: "not endure wrongs any more than gods do" (Riverside, 1,509); **as**: "as do" (Hinman, 82)

Exit

SCENE VI. The same. A banqueting-room in Timon's house.

Music. Tables set out: Servants attending. Enter divers Lords, Senators and

others, at several doors

Several: "separate" (Bevington)

FIRST LORD

1 The good time of day to you, sir.

SECOND LORD

2 I also wish it to you. I think this honorable lord

3 did but try us this other day.

Try: "test" (Mowat, 104)

FIRST LORD

4 Upon that were my thoughts tiring, when we

Tiring: "eagerly feeding (term from falconry" (Riverside, 1,509); "toiling" (Wright, 54)

5 encountered: I hope it is not so low with him as

Encountered: "met"; **it is . . . him**: "his financial situation is not so desperate" (Bevington)

6 he made it seem in the trial of his several friends.

SECOND LORD

7 It should not be, by the persuasion of his new feasting. **By the persuasion**: "on the evidence" (Riverside, 1,509)

FIRST LORD

8 I should think so: he hath sent me an earnest

9 inviting, which many my near occasions did urge me **Inviting**: "invitation" (Mowat, 104); **many**: "many of" (Williams, 52); **near occasions**: "pressing engagements" (Riverside, 1,509)

131

10 to put off; but he hath conjur'd me beyond them, | **Put off**: "decline";
and | **conjur'd . . . them**: "summoned me with an urgency exceeding theirs" (Riverside, 1,509)

11 I must needs appear. | **Needs**: "of necessity" (Mowat, 104)

SECOND LORD

12 In like manner was I in debt to my importunate | **In debt to**: "subject to the demands of" (Riverside, 1,509); **importunate**: "pressing" (Wright, 54)

13 business, but he would not hear my excuse. I am

14 sorry, when he sent to borrow of me, that my

15 provision was out. | **Provision**: "supply (of money)" (Charney, 97); **out**: "exhausted" (Riverside, 1,509)

FIRST LORD

16 I am sick of that grief too, as I understand how all | **How . . . go**: "the way things really are" (Riverside, 1,509)

17 things go.

SECOND LORD

18 Every man here's so. What would he have borrowed of

19 you?

FIRST LORD

20 A thousand pieces. | **Pieces**: "i.e., coins" (Mowat, 104)

SECOND LORD

21 A thousand pieces!

FIRST LORD

22 What of you?

SECOND LORD

23 He sent to me, sir--Here he comes.

Enter TIMON and Attendants

TIMON

24 With all my heart, gentlemen both; and how fare you? **With . . . heart**: "my cordial greetings" (Riverside, 1,509)

FIRST LORD

25 Ever at the best, hearing well of your lordship.

SECOND LORD

26 The swallow follows not summer more willing than we

Swallow: "(cf. the proverb: 'Swallows, like false friends, fly away upon the approach of winter')" (Charney, 98); **willing**: "i.e., willingly" (Mowat, 104)

27 your lordship.

TIMON

28 [Aside] Nor more willingly leaves winter; such

Nor . . . men: "Proverbial: 'Swallows, like false friends, fly away upon the approach of **winter**.'" (Mowat, 106)

29 summer-birds are men. Gentlemen, our dinner will not

30 recompense this long stay: feast your ears with the

Stay: "wait" (Riverside, 1,509)

31 music awhile, if they will fare so harshly o' the

Fare . . . o': "partake of such rough fare as" (Riverside, 1,509)

32 trumpet's sound; we shall to 't presently.

Shall to 't: "i.e., sit down to feast" (Mowat, 106)

FIRST LORD

33 I hope it remains not unkindly with your lordship   **It remains . . .
messenger**: "you don't
harbor unkind thoughts
toward me because I sent
your man back without
any money" (Hinman, 84)

34 that I returned you an empty messenger.   **Empty**: "i.e., empty-
handed" (Mowat, 106)

TIMON

35 O, sir, let it not trouble you.

SECOND LORD

36 My noble lord--

TIMON

37 Ah, my good friend, what cheer?   **What cheer**: "how are
you" (Mowat, 106)

SECOND LORD

38 My most honorable lord, I am e'en sick of shame,   **E'en**: "quite" (Bevington)

39 that, when your lordship this other day sent to me,

40 I was so unfortunate a beggar.   **So . . . beggar**: "so
unlucky as to be out of
money" (Riverside, 1,509)

TIMON

41 Think not on 't, sir.

SECOND LORD

42 If you had sent but two hours before--

TIMON

43 Let it not cumber your better remembrance.   **Cumber . . .
remembrance**: "interfere
with happier memories"
(Riverside, 1,509)

The banquet brought in

44 Come, bring in all together.

SECOND LORD

45 All cover'd dishes!

Cover'd dishes: "promising particularly good food" (Riverside, 1,509)

FIRST LORD

46 Royal cheer, I warrant you.

Royal: "fit for royalty" (Bevington)

THIRD LORD

47 Doubt not that, if money and the season can yield it.

FIRST LORD

48 How do you? What's the news?

THIRD LORD

49 Alcibiades is banished: hear you of it?

FIRST LORD SECOND LORD

50 Alcibiades banished!

THIRD LORD

51 'Tis so, be sure of it.

FIRST LORD

52 How! how!

SECOND LORD

53 I pray you, upon what?

Upon what: "for what cause" (Riverside, 1,509)

TIMON

54 My worthy friends, will you draw near?

THIRD LORD

55 I'll tell you more anon. Here's a noble feast toward.

Anon: "soon" (Bevington); **toward**: "forthcoming" (Riverside, 1,509)

SECOND LORD

56 This is the old man still.

> **Old**: "long-familiar"
> (Mowat, 106); **still**:
> "ever, without change"
> (Charney, 99)

THIRD LORD

57 Will 't hold? will 't hold?

> **Hold**: "last" (Riverside,
> 1,509)

SECOND LORD

58 It does: but time will--and so--

> **Will**: "i.e., will tell"
> (Riverside, 1,509)

THIRD LORD

59 I do conceive.

> **Conceive**: "understand
> you" (Riverside, 1,509)

TIMON

60 Each man to his stool, with that spur as he would to

> **Spur**: "speed"
> (Wright, 56)

61 the lip of his mistress: your diet shall be in all

> **Your diet . . . alike**: "i.e.,
> you will all be served the
> same food" (Mowat, 108)

62 places alike. Make not a city feast of it, to let

> **A city feast**: "an official
> banquet (with seating
> strictly by rank)"
> (Riverside, 1,509)

63 the meat cool ere we can agree upon the first place:

> **Meat**: "food" (Mowat,
> 108); **first place**: "place of
> honor" (Bevington)

64 sit, sit. The gods require our thanks.

65 You great benefactors, sprinkle our society with

> **Society**: "company"
> (Mowat, 108)

66 thankfulness. For your own gifts, make yourselves

67 praised: but reserve still to give, lest your

> **Reserve still**: "always
> keep back (something"
> (Riverside, 1,509)

68 deities be despised. Lend to each man enough, that **Lend**: "give"; **that**: "so that" (Wright, 56)

69 one need not lend to another; for, were your **Were ... gods**: "i.e., even the gods would be forsaken if they became debtors" (Wright, 56)

70 godheads to borrow of men, men would forsake the

71 gods. Make the meat be beloved more than the man

72 that gives it. Let no assembly of twenty be without

73 a score of villains: if there sit twelve women at

74 the table, let a dozen of them be--as they are. The **As they are**: "and what they are goes without saying" (Wright, 56)

75 rest of your fees, O gods--the senators of Athens, **Fees**: "property (?) or those who hold their lives in fee from you (?)" (Riverside, 1,509)

76 together with the common lag of people--what is **Common lag**: "lowest class" (Williams, 55)

77 amiss in them, you gods, make suitable for

78 destruction. For these my present friends, as they **For**: "as for" (Riverside, 1,509)

79 are to me nothing, so in nothing bless them, and to

80 nothing are they welcome.

81 Uncover, dogs, and lap.

The dishes are uncovered and seen to be full of warm water

SOME SPEAK

82 What does his lordship mean?

SOME OTHERS

83 I know not.

TIMON

84 May you a better feast never behold,

Donald J. Richardson

85 You knot of mouth-friends! Smoke and lukewarm water	**Knot**: "company, crowd" (Bevington); **mouth-friends**: "friends won by being fed (cf. *trencher-friends* line 93) (?) or people falsely professing friendship (?)"; **Smoke**: "steam; as applied to the false friends, 'hot air'" (Riverside, 1,510)
86 Is your perfection. This is Timon's last;	**Your perfection**: "what suits you best" (Riverside, 1,510)
87 Who, stuck and spangled with your flatteries,	**Stuck and spangled**: "bespattered and decorated" (Bevington)
88 Washes it off, and sprinkles in your faces	
89 Your reeking villany.	**Reeking**: "smoking, steaming" (Wright, 57)
Throwing the water in their faces	
90 Live loathed and long,	
91 Most smiling, smooth, detested parasites,	**Smooth**: "flattering" (Charney, 101); **detested**: "detestable" (Riverside, 1,510)
92 Courteous destroyers, affable wolves, meek bears,	
93 You fools of fortune, trencher-friends, time's flies,	**Fools of fortune**: "creatures completely controlled (like puppets) by fortune; *fools* = playthings"; **time's flies**: "i.e. creatures who come only in summer, when times are good (cf. II.ii.185-86)" (Riverside, 1,511); **trencher-friends**: "friends only while being fed" (Bevington)

94 Cap-and-knee slaves, vapors, and minute-jacks! | **Cap-and-knee slaves**: "base fellows always rising their hats and bowing"; **minute-jacks**: "time-servers (a jack was the figure striking the bell in a clock)" (Riverside, 1,510); **vapors**: "substanceless creatures" (Bevington)

95 Of man and beast the infinite malady | **Of . . . malady**: "may the worst malady afflicting man or beast" (Wright, 57); **infinite**: "unlimited" (Charney, 101)

96 Crust you quite o'er! What, dost thou go? | **Crust**: "cover with scabs" (Riverside, 1,510)

97 Soft! take thy physic first--thou too--and thou;-- | **Soft**: "wait"; **physic**: "medicine" (Mowat, 110)

98 Stay, I will lend thee money, borrow none. | **Borrow**: "i.e., borrow none from others (?) I will borrow none (?)" (Charney, 101)

Throws the dishes at them, and drives them out

99 What, all in motion? Henceforth be no feast,

100 Whereat a villain's not a welcome guest.

101 Burn, house! sink, Athens! henceforth hated be

102 Of Timon man and all humanity! | **Of**: "by" (Riverside, 1,510)

Exit

Re-enter the Lords, Senators, & c

FIRST LORD

103 How now, my lords!

SECOND LORD

104 Know you the quality of Lord Timon's fury?

Quality: "occasion, cause" (Riverside, 1,510)

THIRD LORD

105 Push! did you see my cap?

Push: "pish, pshaw" (Riverside, 1,510)

FOURTH LORD

106 I have lost my gown.

FIRST LORD

107 He's but a mad lord, and nought but humor sways him.

Mad: "given to mad tricks (but the word means 'insane' in line 114)"; **nought . . . him**: "he is governed wholly by caprice" (Riverside, 1,510)

108 He gave me a jewel th' other day, and now he has

109 beat it out of my hat: did you see my jewel?

THIRD LORD

110 Did you see my cap?

SECOND LORD

111 Here 'tis.

FOURTH LORD

112 Here lies my gown.

FIRST LORD

113 Let's make no stay.

Stay: "delay" (Mowat, 110)

SECOND LORD

114 Lord Timon's mad.

THIRD LORD

115 I feel 't upon my bones.

Upon: "i.e., in"
(Wright, 58)

FOURTH LORD

116 One day he gives us diamonds, next day stones.

Exeunt

ACT IV

SCENE I. Without the walls of Athens.

Enter TIMON

TIMON

1 Let me look back upon thee. O thou wall,

2 That girdlest in those wolves, dive in the earth,

3 And fence not Athens! Matrons, turn incontinent! **Fence**: "(1) enclose (2) defend" (Bevington); **turn incontinent**: "become unchaste" (Mowat, 114)

4 Obedience fail in children! slaves and fools, **Obedience fail**: "let obedience fail" (Bevington)

5 Pluck the grave wrinkled senate from the bench,

6 And minister in their steads! to general filths **Minister**: "administer, i.e., govern" (Mowat, 114); **general filths**: "common prostitutes" (Riverside, 1,510)

7 Convert o' the instant, green virginity, **Convert**: "change (intransitive)"; **green virginity**: "young virgins" (Riverside, 1,510)

8 Do 't in your parents' eyes! bankrupts, hold fast;

9 Rather than render back, out with your knives, **Render back**: "repay" (Wright, 59)

10 And cut your trusters' throats! bound servants, steal! **Your trusters' throats**: "i.e., the **throats** of those who trusted you" (Mowat, 114); **bound**: "under bond to serve for a specified term" (Riverside, 1,510)

11 Large-handed robbers your grave masters are, **Large-handed**: "taking without restraint" (Riverside, 1,510); **grave**: "dignified" (Wright, 59)

12 And pill by law. Maid, to thy master's bed; **Pill**: "plunder" (Riverside, 1,510); **to**: "go to" (Bevington)

13 Thy mistress is o' the brothel! Son of sixteen,

14 pluck the lin'd crutch from thy old limping sire, **Lin'd**: "padded" (Riverside, 1,510)

15 With it beat out his brains! Piety, and fear, **Fear**: "religious awe" (Riverside, 1,510)

16 Religion to the gods, peace, justice, truth, **Religion to**: "reverence for" (Riverside, 1,510)

17 Domestic awe, night-rest, and neighborhood, **Domestic awe**: "respect due to parents and seniors in the family"; **neighborhood**: "neighborly feeling" (Riverside, 1,510)

18 Instruction, manners, mysteries, and trades, **Manners**: "morals" (Mowat, 114); **mysteries**: "trades, crafts" (Riverside, 1,510)

19 Degrees, observances, customs, and laws, **Degrees**: "ranks" (Riverside, 1,510); **observances**: "ceremonies" (Wright, 59)

20 Decline to your confounding contraries,

Decline to: "sink or descend into" (Mowat, 114); **confounding contraries**: "opposites that will produce chaos (*confound* = ruin utterly)" (Riverside, 1,510)

21 And yet confusion live! Plagues, incident to men,

Yet confusion live: "nevertheless (though everything is destroyed) let destruction continue" (Riverside, 1,510); **incident to**: "natural to" (Charney, 104)

22 Your potent and infectious fevers heap

23 On Athens, ripe for stroke! Thou cold sciatica,

Ripe for stroke: "i.e., ready to be struck" (Mowat, 114); **cold**: "i.e. incident to age (?)" (Riverside, 1,510); **sciatica**: "nerve pain in hip and leg" (Bevington)

24 Cripple our senators, that their limbs may halt

Halt: "limp" (Riverside, 1,510)

25 As lamely as their manners. Lust and liberty

Lust and liberty: "licentious freedom" (Wright, 60)

26 Creep in the minds and marrows of our youth,

Marrows: "soft tissues filling the cavities of bone (thought of as the source of vitality and strength)" (Bevington)

27 That 'gainst the stream of virtue they may strive,

Stream: "current"; **strive**: "struggle (to swim)" (Riverside, 1,510)

28 And drown themselves in riot! Itches, blains,

Riot: "licentious living"; **blains**: "sores, blisters"(Riverside, 1,510)

29 Sow all the Athenian bosoms; and their crop

Sow: "sow themselves in" (Riverside, 1,510)

30 Be general leprosy! Breath infect breath,

31 at their society, as their friendship, may

Their: "i.e. the Athenians'"; **society**: "association with one another" (Riverside, 1,510)

32 merely poison! Nothing I'll bear from thee,

Merely: "entirely"; **bear**: "carry away" (Riverside, 1,510)

33 But nakedness, thou detestable town!

Detestable: "with accents on the first and third syllables" (Mowat, 116)

34 Take thou that too, with multiplying bans!

That too: "He is tearing off his clothes." (Riverside, 1,510); **multiplying bans**: "ever-increasing curses (?) multiple curses (?)" (Charney, 104)

35 Timon will to the woods; where he shall find

Will; "i.e., **will** go" (Mowat, 116)

36 The unkindest beast more kinder than mankind.

More kinder: "(1) **more** natural; (2) **more** friendly or benevolent" (Mowat, 116)

37 The gods confound--hear me, you good gods all—

Confound: "destroy, utterly defeat" (Mowat, 116)

38 The Athenians both within and out that wall!

Out: "without" (Williams, 58)

39 And grant, as Timon grows, his hate may grow

Grows: "ages" (Mowat, 116)

40 To the whole race of mankind, high and low! Amen.

Exit

SCENE II. Athens. A room in Timon's house.

Enter FLAVIUS, with two or three Servants

FIRST SERVANT

1 Hear you, master steward, where's our master?

2 Are we undone? cast off? nothing remaining?

> **Undone**: "ruined"; **cast off**: "abandoned" (Mowat, 116)

FLAVIUS

3 Alack, my fellows, what should I say to you?

> **Alack**: "an expression of sorrow"; **fellows**: "comrades, companions, co-workers (with the added meaning of 'equals, peers')" (Mowat, 116)

4 Let me be recorded by the righteous gods,

> **Be recorded by**: "say in the hearing of" (Bevington)

5 I am as poor as you.

FIRST SERVANT

6 Such a house broke!

> **Broke**: "ruined, destroyed" (Mowat, 116); "bankrupt" (Wright, 61)

7 So noble a master fall'n! All gone! and not

8 One friend to take his fortune by the arm,

> **His fortune**: "i.e. him in his ill-fortune" (Riverside, 1,511)

9 And go along with him!

SECOND SERVANT

10 As we do turn our backs

11 From our companion thrown into his grave,

> **From . . . grave**: "from the grave of a newly buried friend" (Hinman, 89)

12 So his familiars to his buried fortunes

**His familiars ...
fortunes**: "those friends
who were so close to
his fortunes now dead"
(Riverside, 1,511)

13 Slink all away, leave their false vows with him,

14 Like empty purses pick'd; and his poor self,

15 A dedicated beggar to the air,

Dedicated ... air: "i.e.
beggar dedicated, or
solely devoted, to the open
air" (Riverside, 1,511)

16 With his disease of all-shunn'd poverty,

17 Walks, like contempt, alone. More of our fellows.

Like contempt: "as if
he were contemptibility
itself"; **fellows**: "fellow
workers, associates (as
also in lines 20, 25, 28)"
(Riverside, 1,511)

Enter other Servants

FLAVIUS

18 All broken implements of a ruin'd house.

Implements: "fittings"
(Wright, 61)

THIRD SERVANT

19 Yet do our hearts wear Timon's livery;

Livery: "uniform,
symbolizing service"
(Wright, 61)

20 That see I by our faces; we are fellows still,

Fellows: "comrades"
(Wright, 61)

21 Serving alike in sorrow: leak'd is our bark,

Bark: "sailing vessel"
(Bevington)

22 And we, poor mates, stand on the dying deck,

Mates: "comrades (with
wordplay on **mates** as
ship's officers" (Mowat,
118); **dying**: "sinking"
(Riverside, 1,511)

23 Hearing the surges threat: we must all part

Surges: "waves" (Bevington); **threat**: "threaten" (Mowat, 118); **part . . . air**: "depart into this expanse of nothingness, death" (Hinman, 90)

24 Into this sea of air.

This sea of air: "i.e., the open air, which is as comfortless to us as is the sea to sailors on a sinking ship" (Charney, 106)

FLAVIUS

25 Good fellows all,

26 The latest of my wealth I'll share amongst you.

Latest: "last" (Riverside, 1,511)

27 Wherever we shall meet, for Timon's sake,

28 Let's yet be fellows; let's shake our heads, and say,

Yet: "still"; **shake our heads**: "(in sorrow)" (Bevington)

29 As 'twere a knell unto our master's fortunes,

Knell: "tolling of a bell, announcing a death or other misfortune" (Bevington)

30 "We have seen better days." Let each take some;

31 Nay, put out all your hands. Not one word more:

All your hands: "the hands of all of you" (Riverside, 1,511)

32 Thus part we rich in sorrow, parting poor.

Servants embrace, and part several ways

Several ways: "in different directions" (Williams, 59)

33 O, the fierce wretchedness that glory brings us!

Fierce: "merciless, violent" (Mowat, 118); **glory**: "greatness, high estate" (Riverside, 1,511)

34 Who would not wish to be from wealth exempt,

35 Since riches point to misery and contempt?   **Point**: "lead" (Wright, 62)

36 Who would be so mock'd with glory? or to live   **Mock'd**: "deluded (by its falsity" (Wright, 62); **to live**: "i.e., who would wish to live" (Charney, 106)

37 But in a dream of friendship?

38 To have his pomp and all what state compounds   **What . . . compounds**: "that splendor is composed of" (Riverside, 1,511); **state**: "pomp, high status, wealth" (Mowat, 118)

39 But only painted, like his varnish'd friends?   **But only**: "nothing more than" (Bevington); **varnish'd**: "simulated, pretended" (Mowat, 118); **painted**: "illusory" (Charney, 106)

40 Poor honest lord, brought low by his own heart,

41 Undone by goodness! Strange, unusual blood,   **Blood**: "nature" (Riverside, 1,511)

42 When man's worst sin is, he does too much good!

43 Who, then, dares to be half so kind again?   **Half so kind**: "i.e., as Timon was, who came to grief because of it" (Charney, 106); **again**: "i.e. in future" (Riverside, 1,511)

44 For bounty, that makes gods, do still mar men.   **Bounty**: "generosity" (Bevington); **makes gods**: "is the very composition of the gods" (Wright, 62); **do**: "i.e., does" (Mowat, 120)

45 My dearest lord, bless'd, to be most accursed,

To be: "only to be" (Bevington)

46 Rich, only to be wretched, thy great fortunes

47 Are made thy chief afflictions. Alas, kind lord!

48 He's flung in rage from this ingrateful seat

Seat: "residence" (Charney, 106)

49 Of monstrous friends, nor has he with him to

Monstrous: "unnatural" (Williams, 60); **to . . . life**: "i.e. what is necessary to sustain life" (Riverside, 1,511)

50 Supply his life, or that which can command it.

That . . . it: "i.e., money" (Bevington); **command**: "secure" (Mowat, 120)

51 I'll follow and inquire him out:

52 I'll ever serve his mind with my best will;

Serve his mind: "execute his wishes" (Bevington)

53 Whilst I have gold, I'll be his steward still.

Exit

SCENE III. Woods and cave, near the seashore.

Enter TIMON, from the cave

1 O blessed breeding sun, draw from the earth

From the earth: "i.e. out of the earth and into the air (to infect the atmosphere)" (Riverside, 1,511)

2 Rotten humidity; below thy sister's orb

Rotten humidity: "dampness that causes rot"; **thy sister's**: "i.e. the moon's. See note on I.i.55." (Riverside, 1,511)

3 Infect the air! Twinn'd brothers of one womb,

4 Whose procreation, residence, and birth,

5 Scarce is dividant, touch them with several fortunes;

Scarce: "i.e., scarcely" (Mowat, 120); **dividant**: "capable of differentiation"; **touch**: "test"; **several**: "different" (Riverside, 1,511)

6 The greater scorns the lesser: not nature,

The greater: "i.e., then the more fortunate" (Mowat, 120); **not . . . nature**: "human nature, subject to all kinds of evils, cannot bear prosperity without behaving in a manner which shows its contempt for the merely natural; i.e. a man raised by fortune out of the normal miseries of nature despises those who continue in them." (Riverside, 1,511)

7 To whom all sores lay siege, can bear great fortune,

To whom . . . siege: "i.e., which is subject to all kinds of suffering" (Mowat, 120)

8 But by contempt of nature.

Contempt of nature: "i.e., being contemptuous **of nature**" (Mowat, 120)

9 Raise me this beggar, and deny 't that lord;

Raise me: "i.e., raise (The word **me** is an ethical dative that does not affect sense but enlivens the expression.)" (Mowat, 120) **deny 't**: "withhold such advancement from. Some editors emend to *deject*." (Riverside, 1,511)

10 The senator shall bear contempt hereditary,

The senator . . . honor: "i.e. the senator will be scorned and the beggar honored, as if each had been born to his new station" (Riverside, 1,511); **hereditary:** "as though baseborn" (Wright, 63)

11 The beggar native honor.

Native honor: "i.e., the **honor** enjoyed by those born into high rank" (Mowat, 122)

12 It is the paster lards the rother's sides,

It . . . lean: "i.e. that one brother prospers and the other does not, is entirely explained by the quality of their luck. Many editors follow Singer in adopting Collier's famous conjecture *rother's*(= ox's) for *brother's*; other, with Warburton, read *wether's*."; **paster:** "pasture" (Riverside, 1,511); **lards . . . sides:** "fattens the sheep" (Hinman, 91)

13 The want that makes him lean. Who dares? who dares,

Want: "lack (of good pasture)" (Bevington)

14 In purity of manhood stand upright,

15 And say "This man's a flatterer?" if one be,

16 So are they all; for every grize of fortune

Grize: "i.e., step in a staircase (or, in this context, the person occupying the step)" (Mowat,122); **every . . . below**: "each rank is flattered by the next lower one" (Hinman, 92)

17 Is smooth'd by that below: the learned pate

Smooth'd: "flattered" (Riverside, 1,511); **pate**: "head" (Bevington)

18 Ducks to the golden fool: all is obliquy;

Ducks: "bows"; **golden**: "rich" (Riverside, 1,511); **obliquy**: "obliquity, or deviation from proper conduct" (Mowat, 122)

19 There's nothing level in our cursed natures,

Level: "direct (with possible wordplay on the sense 'not oblique')" (Mowat, 122)

20 But direct villany. Therefore, be abhorr'd

Direct: "downright (again with possible wordplay on the sense 'not oblique'" (Mowat, 122)

21 All feasts, societies, and throngs of men!

Societies: "companies" (Mowat, 122)

22 His semblable, yea, himself, Timon disdains:

His semblable: "anything resembling him, i.e. his fellow man" (Riverside, 1,511)

23 Destruction fang mankind! Earth, yield me roots! **Fang**: "seize" (Riverside, 1,511)

Digging

24 Who seeks for better of thee, sauce his palate

Of thee: "i.e., from thee" (Mowat, 122); **sauce**: "stimulate, tickle" (Bevington)

25 With thy most operant poison! What is here?

Operant: "potent" (Riverside, 1,511)

26 Gold? yellow, glittering, precious gold? No, gods,

27 I am no idle votarist: roots, you clear heavens!

Idle votarist: "one who makes a vow lightly"; **clear**: "pure" (Riverside, 1,511)

28 Thus much of this will make black white, foul fair,

This: "i.e., gold" (Mowat, 122); **foul**: "ugly" (Riverside, 1,512)

29 Wrong right, base noble, old young, coward valiant.

30 Ha, you gods! why this? what this, you gods? Why, this

What: "for what, why" (Riverside, 1,512)

31 Will lug your priests and servants from your sides,

32 Pluck stout men's pillows from below their heads:

Pluck . . . heads: "'Alludes to the custom of drawing away the pillow to allow a dying man to die more easily. "Stout" implies that gold will hasten on their way even those who are not at their last gasp.' (Warburton, quoted by Maxwell.)" (Riverside, 1,512); **stout**: "strong, hardy" (Mowat, 122)

33 This yellow slave

34 Will knit and break religions, bless the accursed,

Knit . . . religions: "knit men together in religious harmony and then break that harmony apart" (Bevington)

35 Make the hoar leprosy adorcd, place thieves	**Hoar**: "white-skinned" (Bevington); **place**: "give office to" (Riverside, 1,512)
36 And give them title, knee and approbation	**Knee**: "i.e. deference" (Riverside, 1,512)
37 With senators on the bench: this is it	**With**: "i.e. on a level with" (Riverside, 1,512)
38 That makes the wappen'd widow wed again;	**Makes**: "enables" (Bevington); **wappen'd**: "worn-out sexually" (Riverside, 1,512)
39 She, whom the spittle-house and ulcerous sores	**Spittle-house . . . at**: "hospital patients and sufferers from running sores would be sickened by" (Riverside, 1,512); **ulcerous sores**: "i.e., those afflicted with ulcerous sores" (Charney, 108)
40 Would cast the gorge at, this embalms and spices	**Cast . . . at**: "i.e., vomit at the sight of (The image is from falconry: falcons have a **gorge** they fill with food.)" (Mowat, 124); **this . . . again**: "i.e., money enables the diseased old woman to embalm herself with cosmetics to look April-like and marriageable" (Bevington)

41 To th' April day again. Come, damned earth,
To th' April day: "i.e., until she looks and smells like an **April day**"; **earth**: "a disparaging term for precious metals" (Mowat, 124); "i.e., gold" (Bevington)

42 Thou common whore of mankind, that puts odds
Puts . . . nations: "creates dissensions among different peoples" (Riverside, 1,512)

43 Among the rout of nations, I will make thee

44 Do thy right nature.
Do . . . nature: "act in accordance with your true nature, i.e. create trouble" (Riverside, 1,512)

March afar off

45 Ha! a drum? Thou'rt quick,
Quick: "swift in action (with quibble on the sense 'alive')" (Riverside, 1,512)

46 But yet I'll bury thee: thou't go, strong thief,
Thou't: "thou wilt"; **go**: "walk, get about" (Riverside, 1,512); **strong**: "(1) sturdy; (2) confirmed; incorrigible" (Wright, 64)

47 When gouty keepers of thee cannot stand.

48 Nay, stay thou out for earnest.
Earnest: "token payment, pledge" (Riverside, 1,512)

Keeping some gold

Enter ALCIBIADES, with drum and fife, in warlike manner; PHRYNIA and

TIMANDRA
Drum and fife: "i.e., soldiers playing the **drum and fife**" (Mowat, 124)

ALCIBIADES

49 What art thou there? speak.

TIMON

50 A beast, as thou art. The canker gnaw thy heart,

Canker: "ulcerous growth" (Riverside, 1,512); "cancer (or, perhaps, the cankerworm, an insect larva that destroys buds and leaves of plants)" (Mowat, 124)

51 For showing me again the eyes of man!

ALCIBIADES

52 What is thy name? Is man so hateful to thee,

53 That art thyself a man?

TIMON

54 I am Misanthropos, and hate mankind.

Misanthropos: "i.e. a hater of mankind" (Riverside, 1,512)

55 For thy part, I do wish thou wert a dog,

For thy part: "as for you" (Bevington)

56 That I might love thee something.

Something: "a little" (Riverside, 1,512)

ALCIBIADES

57 I know thee well;

58 But in thy fortunes am unlearn'd and strange.

Unlearn'd: "uninformed"; **strange**: "ignorant" (Riverside, 1,512)

TIMON

59 I know thee too; and more than that I know thee,

60 I not desire to know. Follow thy drum;

Not desire: "do not desire" (Bevington)

61 With man's blood paint the ground, gules, gules:

Gules: "red (heraldic term)" (Riverside, 1,512)

62 Religious canons, civil laws are cruel;

Canons: "rules, laws" (Bevington)

63 Then what should war be? This fell whore of thine

Fell: "deadly" (Riverside, 1,512)

64 Hath in her more destruction than thy sword,

65 For all her cherubin look.

Cherubin: "angelic" (Riverside, 1,512)

PHRYNIA

Phrynia: "name is inspired by a famous Athenian courtesan named Phryne" (Asimov, 142)

66 Thy lips rot off!

Thy lips: "may thy lips" (Bevington)

TIMON

67 I will not kiss thee; then the rot returns

Returns: "i.e., stays where it was in the first place" (Wright, 65); **the rot returns**: "(based on a prevalent belief that by transmitting a venereal infection to another, one loses it himself)" (Charney, 110)

68 To thine own lips again.

ALCIBIADES

69 How came the noble Timon to this change?

TIMON

70 As the moon does, by wanting light to give:

Wanting: "lacking" (Riverside, 1,512)

71 But then renew I could not, like the moon;

Renew: "become new again (with a quibble on the idea of renewing a loan)" (Bevington)

72 There were no suns to borrow of.

Suns: "(punning on *sons*, i.e., men)" (Bevington)

ALCIBIADES

73 Noble Timon,

74 What friendship may I do thee?

TIMON

75 None, but to

But: "except" (Riverside, 1,512)

76 Maintain my opinion.

Maintain: "uphold" (Wright, 66); **Maintain my opinion**: "(i.e., be a misanthropist, too [sic]" (Charney, 110)

ALCIBIADES

77 What is it, Timon?

TIMON

78 Promise me friendship, but perform none: if thou

If . . . man: "i.e. if you refuse to make false promises, or if you make promises and carry them out, damn you anyway, because you are a man" (Riverside, 1,512)

79 wilt not promise, the gods plague thee, for thou art

80 a man! if thou dost perform, confound thee, for

Confound thee: "i.e., may you be destroyed" (Mowat, 126)

81 thou art a man!

ALCIBIADES

82 I have heard in some sort of thy miseries.

In some sort: "to some extent" (Riverside, 1,512)

TIMON

83 Thou saw'st them, when I had prosperity.

ALCIBIADES

84 I see them now; then was a blessed time.

TIMON

85 As thine is now, held with a brace of harlots.

Held with: "i.e. bound to" (Riverside, 1,512); **brace**: "pair (with a quibble on the meaning 'clamp,' one that holds Alcibiades in its grip)" (Bevington); "(usually for a pair of dogs on a leash)" (Charney, 110)

TIMANDRA

86 Is this the Athenian minion, whom the world

Minion: "favorite; darling (with contempt)" (Wright, 66)

87 Voic'd so regardfully?

Voic'd so regardfully: "spoke of so respectfully" (Riverside, 1,512)

TIMON

88 Art thou Timandra?

TIMANDRA

89 Yes.

TIMON

90 Be a whore still: they love thee not that use thee;

91 Give them diseases, leaving with thee their lust.

Leaving: "while they are leaving" (Bevington)

92 Make use of thy salt hours: season the slaves

Use: "profit" (Wright, 66); **salt**: "lecherous, salacious (with wordplay on 'condiment,' since **salt** is followed by **Season**, itself a pun on 'fit, prepare' and 'add flavor')" (Mowat, 126)

93 For tubs and baths; bring down rose-cheekcd youth

Tubs . . . diet: "referring to treatments for venereal diseases" (Riverside, 1,512)

94 To the tub-fast and the diet.

Tub-fast: "abstinence during treatment in the sweating-tub"; **the diet**: "i.e., **the** curative **diet**" (Mowat, 126)

TIMANDRA

95 Hang thee, monster!

ALCIBIADES

96 Pardon him, sweet Timandra; for his wits

97 Are drown'd and lost in his calamities.

98 I have but little gold of late, brave Timon,

Brave: "excellent" (Charney, 111)

99 The want whereof doth daily make revolt

Want: "lack"; **make revolt**: "provoke mutiny" (Bevington)

100 In my penurious band: I have heard, and grieved,

Penurious: "needy" (Charney, 111)

101 How cursed Athens, mindless of thy worth,

102 Forgetting thy great deeds, when neighbor states,

Neighbor: "neighboring" (Williams, 64)

103 But for thy sword and fortune, trod upon them—

But . . . fortune: "(A suggestion of Timon's history as a great military leader, for which Athens ought to be grateful.)" (Bevington); **trod**: "would have trodden" (Riverside, 1,512)

TIMON

104 I prithee, beat thy drum, and get thee gone.

> **Beat thy drum**: "let thy drummer give the signal for departure" (Charney, 111)

ALCIBIADES

105 I am thy friend, and pity thee, dear Timon.

TIMON

106 How dost thou pity him whom thou dost trouble?

107 I had rather be alone.

ALCIBIADES

108 Why, fare thee well:

109 Here is some gold for thee.

TIMON

110 Keep it, I cannot eat it.

ALCIBIADES

111 When I have laid proud Athens on a heap--

> **On a heap**: "in ruins" (Riverside, 1,512)

TIMON

112 Warr'st thou 'gainst Athens?

ALCIBIADES

113 Ay, Timon, and have cause.

TIMON

114 The gods confound them all in thy conquest;

> **Confound**: "destroy" (Mowat, 128); **in thy conquest**: "i.e., in your victory over them" (Charney, 112)

115 And thee after, when thou hast conquer'd!

ALCIBIADES

116 Why me, Timon?

TIMON

117 That, by killing of villains,

That . . . country: "(Timon evidently applauds the deed but not the doer. His words are obscure and the text may be corrupt.)" (Bevington)

118 Thou wast born to conquer my country.

119 Put up thy gold: go on--here's gold--go on;

Put up: "put away" (Riverside, 1,513)

120 Be as a planetary plague, when Jove

Planetary: "caused by a malignant planet" (Riverside, 1,513); **Jove**: "in Roman mythology, king of the gods" (Mowat, 128)

121 Will o'er some high-viced city hang his poison

High-viced: "i.e., extremely wicked" (Mowat, 128)

122 In the sick air: let not thy sword skip one:

Sick: "i.e., corrupt" (Mowat, 128); "sick, and thus infectious" (Wright, 67)

123 Pity not honor'd age for his white beard;

124 He is an usurer: strike me the counterfeit matron;

Strike me: "i.e., **strike**; or, perhaps, **strike** for **me**, or **strike** on my behalf" (Mowat, 128); **counterfeit**: "pretending respectability" (Bevington)

125 It is her habit only that is honest,

Habit: "dress, outward behavior" (Riverside, 1,513); **honest**: "chaste" (Mowat, 128)

126 Herself's a bawd: let not the virgin's cheek

127 Make soft thy trenchant sword; for those milk paps, **Trenchant**: "sharp";
milk paps: "nipples"
(Mowat, 128)

128 That through the window-bars bore at men's eyes, **Window-bars**: "lattice
of her window (?) or
open-work squares
of her bodice (?)"
(Riverside, 1,513); **bore
at**: "show themselves to"
(Williams, 65)

129 Are not within the leaf of pity writ, **Within . . . writ**: "i.e. on
the list of things that are
to be spared" (Riverside,
1,513)

130 But set them down horrible traitors: spare not the **Set them down**: "i.e.,
babe, record **them** as" (Mowat,
130); **traitors**: "i.e.,
betrayers of men"
(Bevington)

131 Whose dimpled smiles from fools exhaust their **Exhaust**: "draw out"
mercy; (Riverside, 1,513)

132 Think it a bastard, whom the oracle **Whom**: "who"
(Williams, 65)

133 Hath doubtfully pronounced the throat shall cut, **Doubtfully**: "ambiguously
or obscurely" (Riverside,
1,513); **the . . . cut**:
"perhaps, **shall cut** thy
throat" (Mowat, 130)

134 And mince it sans remorse. Swear against **Mince**: "slash, cut in
objects; small pieces" (Bevington);
sans remorse: "without
pity"; **Swear against
objects**: "take an oath
not to heed objections"
(Riverside, 1,513)

135 Put armor on thine ears and on thine eyes;

136 Whose proof, nor yells of mothers, maids, nor
   babes,

Whose proof: "the impenetrability of which (armor)" (Riverside, 1,513); **nor**: "neither" (Wright, 68)

137 Nor sight of priests in holy vestments bleeding,

138 Shall pierce a jot. There's gold to pay soldiers:

139 Make large confusion; and, thy fury spent,

Large confusion: "widespread destruction" (Riverside, 1,513)

140 Confounded be thyself! Speak not, be gone.

ALCIBIADES

141 Hast thou gold yet? I'll take the gold thou

Hast: "i.e., if you have" (Charney, 113)

142 givest me,

143 Not all thy counsel.

TIMON

144 Dost thou, or dost thou not, heaven's curse

Dost . . . not: "whether you do or not" (Riverside, 1,513)

145 upon thee!

PHRYNIA TIMANDRA

146 Give us some gold, good Timon: hast thou more?

TIMON

147 Enough to make a whore forswear her trade,

Forswear: "i.e. retire from" (Riverside, 1,513)

148 And to make whores, a bawd. Hold up, you sluts,

To . . . bawd: "i.e. make a bawd retire from her trade of turning women into whores" (Riverside, 1,513)

149 Your aprons mountant: you are not oathable,

Mountant: "rising. (A coining on the analogy of such heraldic terms as *rampant*; he means 'hold up your skirts—which you're accustomed enough to doing—to receive the gold.')"; **oathable**: "fit to be trusted on your oath" (Riverside, 1,513)

150 Although, I know, you 'll swear, terribly swear

Swear: "(to do what I shall ask)" (Hinman, 97)

151 Into strong shudders and to heavenly agues

Strong: "severe" (Mowat, 130); **agues**: "feverish shivers" (Bevington)

152 The immortal gods that hear you--spare your oaths,

153 I'll trust to your conditions: be whores still;

Conditions: "vocations or dispositions as whores" (Wright, 68); "characters"; **still**: "always" (Riverside, 1,513)

154 And he whose pious breath seeks to convert you,

155 Be strong in whore, allure him, burn him up;

Strong in whore: "steadfast in remaining whores"; **burn him up**: "i.e., in the fires of lust; and, in the fever of venereal disease" (Mowat, 130)

156 Let your close fire predominate his smoke,

Let ... smoke: "i.e., let the hidden fire of your sexuality of disease dominate over the smoke of idle words of he who 'seeks to convert you'" (Charney, 113); **predominate**: "overmaster"; **his smoke**: "i.e. his 'pious breath.'" (Riverside, 1,513)

157 And be no turncoats: yet may your pains, six
months,

Pains . . . months:
"obscure; perhaps
referring to abnormal
menstrual pain"
(Riverside, 1,513); **yet . . .
contrary**: "i.e., may you
spend six months of the
year in being whores
and the other six in
repairing the physical
damage occasioned by
your debaucheries (?)"
(Charney, 113)

158 Be quite contrary: and thatch your poor thin roofs

Quite contrary: "i.e.,
devoted to attempts to
cure your own infection"
(Wright, 68); **thatch . . .
dead**: "cover your heads
(the hair being lost
through disease) with
wigs made from the hair
of the dead" (Riverside,
1,513)

159 With burthens of the dead--some that were hang'd,

Burthens of the dead:
"false hair from corpses"
(Wright, 68)

160 No matter; wear them, betray with them: whore
still;

Betray with them: "i.e.,
use these wigs to create
false beauty to betray
more men" (Bevington)

161 Paint till a horse may mire upon your face,

Paint . . . face: "i.e.,
apply such a thick coat
of cosmetics that **a horse**
may sink into **your face**
as into muddy ground"
(Mowat, 132); **mire upon**:
"bog down in" (Riverside,
1,513)

162 A pox of wrinkles!

Pox of: "curse on" (Mowat, 132)

PHRYNIA TIMANDRA

163 Well, more gold: what then?

164 Believe't, that we'll do any thing for gold.

TIMON

165 Consumptions sow

Consumptions: "use of all wasting disease, including syphilis" (Riverside, 1,513)

166 In hollow bones of man; strike their sharp shins,

In hollow bones: "i.e. in bones which become hollow in consequence" (Riverside, 1,513); **sharp shins**: "i.e., shinbones afflicted with painful nodes (another symptom of venereal disease)" (Mowat, 132)

167 And mar men's spurring. Crack the lawyer's voice,

Spurring: "i.e., horseback riding (with wordplay on the sex act)" (Mowat, 132)

168 That he may never more false title plead,

169 Nor sound his quillets shrilly: hoar the flamen,

Quillets: "quibbles"; **hoar the flamen**: "whiten (with disease) the priest; with a quibble on *hoar/whore*" (Riverside, 1,513)

170 That scolds against the quality of flesh,

Quality of flesh: "fleshly nature, carnality" (Riverside, 1,513); **flesh**: "sexual intercourse" (Mowat, 132)

171 And not believes himself: down with the nose,

And . . . himself: "i.e., and doesn't practice what he preaches" (Bevington); **down . . . nose**: "The decay of the nasal bone was a conspicuous effect of syphilis." (Riverside, 1,513)

172 Down with it flat; take the bridge quite away

173 Of him that, his particular to foresee,

Particular: "private gain"; **foresee**: "provide for" (Riverside, 1,513)

174 Smells from the general weal: make curl'd-pate

Smells . . . weal: "loses the scent of the public welfare" (Riverside, 1,513); **curl'd pate**: "curly-haired" (Mowat, 132)

175 ruffians bald;

Ruffians: "men who protected prostitutes, often characterized by long hair" (Wright, 69)

176 And let the unscarr'd braggarts of the war

Unscarr'd . . . war: "those who boast of their war service but have no scar to show for it" (Riverside, 1,513)

177 Derive some pain from you: plague all;

178 That your activity may defeat and quell

Quell: "destroy" (Riverside, 1,513)

179 The source of all erection. There's more gold:

Erection: "advancement, invigoration (with wordplay on the sexual sense)" (Mowat, 132)

180 Do you damn others, and let this damn you,

181 And ditches grave you all!

Grave: "enclose in the grave (with a pun on 'ditches' and 'damming' continued from l. 180)" (Bevington)

PHRYNIA TIMANDRA

182 More counsel with more money, bounteous Timon.

TIMON

183 More whore, more mischief first; I have given you earnest.

Whore: "i.e. activity as whore"; **earnest**: "token payment" (Riverside, 1,513); **mischief**: "disease; harm; wickedness" (Mowat, 132); **earnest**: "earnest money, token payment" (Bevington)

ALCIBIADES

184 Strike up the drum towards Athens! Farewell, Timon:

185 If I hope well, I'll visit thee again.

If . . . well: "if my hope is realized" (Riverside, 1,513)

TIMON

186 If I hope well, I'll never see thee more.

Hope well: "attain my hope" (Williams, 67)

ALCIBIADES

187 I never did thee harm.

TIMON

188 Yes, thou spokest well of me.

Spokest well of me: "cf. the proverb 'Praise by evil men is dispraise.'" (Wright, 69)

ALCIBIADES

189 Call'st thou that harm?

TIMON

190 Men daily find it. Get thee away, and take

Find it: "discover that it is" (Riverside, 1,513)

191 Thy beagles with thee.

Beagles: "small, hunting dogs, i.e. the prostitutes" (Riverside, 1,513)

ALCIBIADES

192 We but offend him. Strike!

Strike: "i.e., sound the drum" (Mowat, 134)

Drum beats. Exeunt ALCIBIADES, PHRYNIA, and TIMANDRA

TIMON

193 That nature, being sick of man's unkindness,

That: "to think that" (Bevington); **sick of**: "satiated with" (Riverside, 1,513); **of**: "as a result of" (Charney, 115)

194 Should yet be hungry! Common mother, thou,

Common mother: "i.e., the earth (proverbial)" (Mowat, 134)

Digging

195 Whose womb unmeasurable, and infinite breast,

Whose . . . feeds all: "i.e., **whose unmeasurable womb teems** (i.e. gives birth) and **whose infinite breast feeds all**" (Mowat, 134)

196 Teems, and feeds all; whose self-same mettle,

Teems: "bears" (Riverside, 1,513); **mettle**: "spirit (with wordplay on 'metal,' from which **mettle** had yet to be distinguished in spelling, meaning earthy matter or substance)" (Mowat, 134)

197 Whereof thy proud child, arrogant man, is puff'd, **Whereof**: "with which" (Bevington); **puff'd**: "inflated with pride" (Riverside, 1,514)

198 Engenders the black toad and adder blue,

199 The gilded newt and eyeless venom'd worm, **Eyeless venom'd worm**: "probably the blindworm, wrongly believed to be poisonous" (Riverside, 1,514)

200 With all the abhorred births below crisp heaven **Abhorred**: "abhorrent"; **crisp**: "clear (?) or wavy (with clouds) (?)" (Riverside, 1,514)

201 Whereon Hyperion's quick'ning fire doth shine; **Hyperion**: "the sun"; **quick'ning**: "life-giving" (Riverside, 1,514)

202 Yield him, who all thy human sons do hate, **Who . . . hate**: "who hates all your human offspring" (Bevington)

203 From forth thy plenteous bosom, one poor root!

204 Ensear thy fertile and conceptious womb, **Ensear**: "dry up"; **conceptious**: "conceiving, prolific" (Riverside, 1,514)

205 Let it no more bring out ingrateful man!

206 Go great with tigers, dragons, wolves, and bears; **Go great**: "be pregnant" (Riverside, 1,514)

207 Teem with new monsters, whom thy upward face **Teem**: "be prolific, or fertile"; **upward**: "upturned" (Mowat, 134); **whom . . . presented**: "i.e., hitherto unknown" (Hinman, 99)

208 Hath to the marbled mansion all above

Marbled mansion: "i.e. heaven. *Marbled* is variously explained as 'shining' or 'enduring, changeless.'" (Riverside, 1,514)

209 Never presented!--O, a root--dear thanks!--

Dear: "heartfelt" (Riverside, 1,514)

210 Dry up thy marrows, vines, and plough-torn leas;

Marrows . . . leas: "i.e. the vineyards and fields of grain which can be regarded as the vital strength (*narrows*) of the earth's body" (Riverside, 1,514); **plow-torn leas:** "plowed-up pastureland" (Bevington)

211 Whereof ungrateful man, with liquorish draughts

Liquorish drafts: "delightful drinks (with wordplay on intoxicating liquors)" (Mowat, 134)

212 And morsels unctious, greases his pure mind,

Unctious: "unctuous, richly fat"; **greases:** "makes gross" (Riverside, 1,514)

213 That from it all consideration slips!

That: "i.e., so **that**" (Mowat, 134); **consideration:** "reflection" (Riverside, 1,514); "regard for higher things" (Williams, 68)

Enter APEMANTUS

214 More man? plague, plague!

APEMANTUS

215 I was directed hither: men report

216 Thou dost affect my manners, and dost use them. **Affect my manners**: "i.e., assume or take on my ways of behaving" (Mowat, 134); **affect**: "imitate" (Charney, 116)

TIMON

217 'Tis, then, because thou dost not keep a dog,

218 Whom I would imitate: consumption catch thee! **Would**: "i.e., would in that case"; **consumption catch thee**: "may a wasting illness lay hold on you" (Bevington)

APEMANTUS

219 This is in thee a nature but infected; **But infected**: "i.e., not inborn and philosophical but induced by misery and hence shallow" (Bevington)

220 A poor unmanly melancholy sprung

221 From change of future. Why this spade? this place? **Change of future**: "i.e., change in your material prospects" (Charney, 116)

222 This slave-like habit? and these looks of care? **Habit**: "garb" (Riverside, 1,514)

223 Thy flatterers yet wear silk, drink wine, lie soft;

224 Hug their diseased perfumes, and have forgot **Diseased perfumes**: "diseased and perfumed mistresses" (Charney, 116)

225 That ever Timon was. Shame not these woods,

226 By putting on the cunning of a carper. **Putting on**: "pretending" (Wright, 71); **cunning**: "art, craft"; **carper**: "faultfinder, censorious critic" (Mowat, 136)

227 Be thou a flatterer now, and seek to thrive

228 By that which has undone thee: hinge thy knee, **Undone**: "destroyed" (Mowat, 136)

229 And let his very breath, whom thou'lt observe, **Let his ... cap**: "kneel so obsequiously close to the person you are paying court to that his breath may blow off your cap" (Charney, 116); **observe**: "pay court to" (Riverside, 1,514)

230 Blow off thy cap; praise his most vicious strain, **Blow ... cap**: "Doffing one's **cap** was a mark of deference."; **strain**: "feature of character" (Mowat, 136)

231 And call it excellent: thou wast told thus; **Thou ... thus**: "this is what you used to be told" (Riverside, 1,514)

232 Thou gavest thine ears like tapsters that bid welcome **Ears**: "i.e., attention"; **like ... welcome**: "i.e., like barkeeps who welcome all comers indiscriminately" (Bevington)

233 To knaves and all approachers: 'tis most just **Just**: "suitable, fitting" (Mowat, 136)

234 That thou turn rascal; hadst thou wealth again, **Rascal**: "(1) rogue; (2) deer in poor condition, isolated from the herd" (Riverside, 1,514)

235 Rascals should have 't. Do not assume my likeness. **Rascals ... have 't**: "i.e., he would give it to rascals" (Wright, 71)

TIMON

236 Were I like thee, I'ld throw away myself.

APEMANTUS

237 Thou hast cast away thyself, being like thyself;

238 A madman so long, now a fool. What, think'st

So long: "i.e., for **so long**": (Mowat, 136); **think'st . . . warm**: "(Alludes to the practice of having a servant warm one's garment by the fire)" (Bevington)

239 That the bleak air, thy boisterous chamberlain,

Boisterous chamberlain: "i.e., incompetent or unskilled changer attendant (personal servant), though with wordplay on **boisterous** as stormy (describing the **air**)" (Mowat, 136)

240 Will put thy shirt on warm? will these moist trees,

Moist: "damp" (Charney, 117)

241 That have outlived the eagle, page thy heels,

Eagle: "The **eagle** was proverbially long-lived" (Mowat, 136); **page**: "follow attentively like pages" (Riverside, 1,514)

242 And skip where thou point'st out? will the

Skip . . . out: "i.e. leap to do your bidding" (Riverside, 1,514)

243 cold brook,

244 Candied with ice, caudle thy morning taste,

Candied: "crusted over (as with sugar)"; **caudle . . . taste**: "serve you a warm soothing drink in the morning" (Riverside, 1,514)

245 To cure thy o'er-night's surfeit? Call the creatures

O'er-night's: "last night's" (Riverside, 1,514)

246 Whose naked natures live in all the spite

Naked natures: "naturally naked selves"; **in**: "exposed to" (Wright, 71)

247 Of wreakful heaven, whose bare unhoused trunks,

Wreakful: "vengeful"; **trunks**: "bodies" (Riverside, 1,514)

248 To the conflicting elements exposed,

249 Answer mere nature; bid them flatter thee;

Answer: "stand up to"; **mere nature**: "unmitigated **nature**, or **nature** in all its severity and intensity" (Mowat, 138)

250 O, thou shalt find--

TIMON

251 A fool of thee: depart.

Of: "in" (Riverside, 1,514)

APEMANTUS

252 I love thee better now than e'er I did.

TIMON

253 I hate thee worse.

APEMANTUS

254 Why?

TIMON

255 Thou flatter'st misery.

APEMANTUS

256 I flatter not; but say thou art a caitiff.

Caitiff: "wretch" (Riverside, 1,514)

TIMON

257 Why dost thou seek me out?

177

Donald J. Richardson

APEMANTUS

258 To vex thee.

Vex: "seriously afflict or distress" (Mowat, 138)

TIMON

259 Always a villain's office or a fool's.

Office: "function" (Mowat, 138)

260 Dost please thyself in't?

APEMANTUS

261 Ay.

TIMON

262 What! a knave too?

A knave too: "i.e., as well as a fool, if he enjoys being vexatious" (Wright, 72)

APEMANTUS

263 If thou didst put this sour-cold habit on

Habit: "disposition, demeanor" (Mowat, 138)

264 To castigate thy pride, 'twere well: but thou

'Twere: "it would be" (Wright, 72)

265 Dost it enforcedly; thou'ldst courtier be again,

Enforcedly: "under compulsion" (Mowat, 138)

266 Wert thou not beggar. Willing misery

Willing . . . before: "poverty when voluntarily undergone is a securer state than luxury with all its uncertainties, and achieves its desires sooner" (Riverside, 1,514)

267 Outlives incertain pomp, is crown'd before:

Incertain pomp: "i.e., uncertain splendor"; **is crown'd**: "achieves supreme happiness" (Wright, 72); **before**: "sooner; or, perhaps, in advance, beforehand" (Mowat, 138)

268 The one is filling still, never complete;

The one: "i.e., the life of **incertain pomp**"; **filling still, never complete**: "i.e., always less than contented" (Mowat, 138)

269 The other, at high wish: best state, contentless,

The other . . . wish: "i.e., the life of **willing misery** is perfectly contented" (Mowat, 138); **best state, contentless**: "the highest state, without content" (Wright, 72)

270 Hath a distracted and most wretched being,

271 Worse than the worst, content.

Worse . . . content: "worse than the meanest state which is contentedly accepted" (Riverside, 1,514)

272 Thou shouldst desire to die, being miserable.

Miserable: "discontented" (Hinman, 101)

TIMON

273 Not by his breath that is more miserable.

Not . . . miserable: "i.e., not when he who speaks (Apemantus) is more to be pitied than I" (Bevington); **his breath**: "the advice of him" (Riverside, 1,514); "voice" (Charney, 118)

274 Thou art a slave, whom Fortune's tender arm

275 With favor never clasp'd; but bred a dog.

Bred a dog: "have been a dog from birth" (Hinman, 101)

276 Hadst thou, like us from our first swath, proceeded

Swath: "swaddling-clothes"; **proceeded**: "passed through (university term)" (Riverside, 1,514)

277 The sweet degrees that this brief world affords

Sweet degrees: "pleasing steps (to good fortune)" (Wright, 72)

278 To such as may the passive drugs of it

Passive drugs: "Schmidt explains as 'all things in passive subserviency to salutary as well as pernicious purposes' (since *drug* was frequently used of poison as well as of healing substances); but *drugges* (the reading of F1 was also a variant spelling of *drudges*, which most editors take to be the probably meaning here." (Riverside, 1,514)

279 Freely command, thou wouldst have plunged thyself

280 In general riot; melted down thy youth

General riot: "wholesale dissipation" (Mowat, 140)

281 In different beds of lust; and never learn'd

Different: "various" (Mowat, 140)

282 The icy precepts of respect, but follow'd

Icy . . . respect: "the cold admonitions of reason" (Riverside, 1,514)

283 The sugar'd game before thee. But myself,

Sugar'd game: "enticing quarry" (Riverside, 1,515)

284 Who had the world as my confectionary,

Confectionary: "place where sweets are made" (Riverside, 1,515)

285 The mouths, the tongues, the eyes and hearts of men

286 At duty, more than I could frame employment,

At duty: "awaiting my command"; **frame**: "devise (for)" (Riverside, 1,515)

287 That numberless upon me stuck as leaves

That: "i.e. they that" (Riverside, 1,515); **numberless**: "innumerable" (Wright, 73); **stuck**: "having stuck" (Bevington)

288 Do on the oak, have with one winter's brush

Have: "i.e., and now have" (Williams, 71); **winter's brush**: "gust of wintry wind" (Bevington)

289 Fell from their boughs and left me open, bare

Fell: "fallen" (Riverside, 1,515); **open**: "exposed" (Bevington)

290 For every storm that blows: I, to bear this,

I . . . this: "that I should bear this" (Bevington)

291 That never knew but better, is some burden:

That . . . better: "who have known only better fortune" (Bevington)

292 Thy nature did commence in sufferance, time

Sufferance: "suffering" (Riverside, 1,515)

293 Hath made thee hard in't. Why shouldst thou hate men?

Made . . . in't: "hardened you to it" (Riverside, 1,515)

294 They never flatter'd thee: what hast thou given?

295 If thou wilt curse, thy father, that poor rag,

Rag: "i.e., wretch" (Bevington)

296 Must be thy subject, who in spite put stuff

In spite: "maliciously"; **Put stuff / To**: "i.e., copulated with" (Mowat, 140)

297 To some she beggar and compounded thee

Compounded: "composed" (Mowat, 140); "begot" (Bevington)

298 Poor rogue hereditary. Hence, be gone!

Hereditary: "by natural inheritance" (Mowat, 140)

299 If thou hadst not been born the worst of men,

Worst: "basest" (Wright, 73)

300 Thou hadst been a knave and flatterer.

APEMANTUS

301 Art thou proud yet?

Yet: "still" (Mowat, 140)

TIMON

302 Ay, that I am not thee.

APEMANTUS

303 Ay, that I was

304 No prodigal.

TIMON

305 I, that I am one now:

306 Were all the wealth I have shut up in thee,

Shut up in: "confined to" (Wright, 73)

307 I'ld give thee leave to hang it. Get thee gone.

Hang it: "i.e., hang yourself" (Bevington)

308 That the whole life of Athens were in this!

That the: "i.e. I wish **that the**" (Mowat, 140)

309 Thus would I eat it.

Eating a root

APEMANTUS

310 Here; I will mend thy feast.

Mend: "improve" (Riverside, 1,515)

Offering him a root

TIMON

311 First mend my company, take away thyself.

APEMANTUS

312 So I shall mend mine own, by the lack of thine.

TIMON

313 'Tis not well mended so, it is but botch'd;

> **'Tis not**: "i.e., your company is not" (Mowat, 142); **botch'd**: "badly mended (because he is still in his own company)" (Riverside, 1,515)

314 if not, I would it were.

> **If . . . were**: "Obscure; perhaps 'I wish your company were truly mended—by your death.'" (Riverside, 1,515)

APEMANTUS

315 What wouldst thou have to Athens?

> **What . . . have**: "i.e. what report shall I take back, what message will you send (but Timon replies with a quibble)" (Riverside, 1,515)

TIMON

316 Thee thither in a whirlwind. If thou wilt,

317 Tell them there I have gold; look, so I have.

APEMANTUS

318 Here is no use for gold.

TIMON

319 The best and truest;

320 For here it sleeps, and does no hired harm.

> **Hired**: "suborned" (Riverside, 1,515)

APEMANTUS

321 Where liest a' nights, Timon?

A' nights: "at night" (Mowat, 142)

TIMON

322 Under that's above me.

That's: "what is" (Riverside, 1,515)

323 Where feed'st thou a' days, Apemantus?

A'days: "during the day" (Mowat, 142)

APEMANTUS

324 Where my stomach finds meat; or, rather,

Meat: "food" (Mowat, 142)

325 where I eat it.

TIMON

326 Would poison were obedient and knew my mind!

Would: "i.e., I wish" (Mowat, 142)

APEMANTUS

327 Where wouldst thou send it?

TIMON

328 To sauce thy dishes.

Sauce: "flavor" (Bevington)

APEMANTUS

329 The middle of humanity thou never knewest, but the

The middle of humanity: "(1) the average state of human fortune; (2) moderation of temper" (Wright, 74)

330 extremity of both ends: when thou wast in thy gilt

Gilt: "gold" (Mowat, 142)

331 and thy perfume, they mocked thee for too much

332 curiosity; in thy rags thou knowest none, but art

Curiosity: "fastidiousness" (Riverside, 1,515)

333 despised for the contrary. There's a medlar for

Medlar: "fruit like a small brown-skinned apple, eaten when nearly decayed; used here, as often, for the sake of a quibble on *meddler*, with sexual suggestion" (Bevington)

334 thee, eat it.

TIMON

335 On what I hate I feed not.

APEMANTUS

336 Dost hate a medlar?

Hate: "('eat' and 'hate' were pronounced alike in Elizabethan English)" (Charney, 121)

TIMON

337 Ay, though it look like thee.

Like thee: "i.e., in a state of decay, or as one who meddles" (Bevington)

APEMANTUS

338 And thou hadst hated meddlers sooner, thou shouldst

And: "if" (Riverside, 1,515); **meddlers**: "(1) the fruit (2) busybodies, intriguers (3) those who overindulge in sexual intercourse" (Charney, 121)

339 have loved thyself better now. What man didst thou

340 ever know unthrift that was beloved after his means?

Unthrift: "i.e., as a spendthrift or prodigal" (Mowat, 142); **after**: "(1) in accordance with; (2) after the loss of" (Riverside, 1,515)

TIMON

341 Who, without those means thou talkest of, didst thou

342 ever know beloved?

APEMANTUS

343 Myself.

TIMON

344 I understand thee; thou hadst some

> **Thou … dog**: "i.e. since only a dog could love you, you must once have had means enough to keep a dog" (Riverside, 1,515)

345 means to keep a dog.

APEMANTUS

346 What things in the world canst thou nearest

347 compare to thy flatterers?

TIMON

348 Women nearest; but men, men are the things

349 themselves. What wouldst thou do with the world,

350 Apemantus, if it lay in thy power?

APEMANTUS

351 Give it the beasts, to be rid of the men.

TIMON

352 Wouldst thou have thyself fall in the confusion of

> **The confusion of men**: "i.e., the original Fall in the Garden of Eden" (Charney, 121); **confusion**: "ruin" (Williams, 73)

353 men, and remain a beast with the beasts?

APEMANTUS

354 Ay, Timon.

TIMON

355 A beastly ambition, which the gods grant thee t'

356 attain to! If thou wert the lion, the fox would

357 beguile thee; if thou wert the lamb, the fox would   **Beguile**: "deceive by craft" (Riverside, 1,515)

358 eat thee: if thou wert the fox, the lion would

359 suspect thee, when peradventure thou wert accused by   **Peradventure**: "perchance" (Mowat, 144); **when . . . wert**: "if you happened to be" (Riverside, 1,515)

360 the ass: if thou wert the ass, thy dullness would

361 torment thee, and still thou liv'dst but as a   **Liv'dst**: "wouldst live" (Riverside, 1,515)

362 breakfast to the wolf: if thou wert the wolf, thy

363 greediness would afflict thee, and oft thou shouldst

364 hazard thy life for thy dinner: wert thou the

365 unicorn, pride and wrath would confound thee and   **Unicorn**: "caught by being tricked into charging a tree and embedding its horn deeply" (Riverside, 1,515); **confound**: "destroy" (Mowat, 144)

366 make thine own self the conquest of thy fury: wert

367 thou a bear, thou wouldst be killed by the horse: **Horse**: "the horse's hostility to the bear was reported by Edward Topsell in his *History of Four-Footed Beasts* (1607)" (Wright, 76)

368 wert thou a horse, thou wouldst be seized by the

369 leopard: wert thou a leopard, thou wert germane to   **Wert germane**: "wouldst be german, i.e. akin, related" (Riverside, 1,515)

187

370 the lion and the spots of thy kindred were jurors on

The spots . . . life: "the crimes of your relatives would be reasons for condemning you to death" (Riverside, 1,515); **were jurors on**: "i.e., would sit in judgment **on**" (Mowat, 144)

371 thy life: all thy safety were remotion and thy

All . . . remotion: "your only safety would lie in removing yourself to some other place" (Riverside, 1,515)

372 defense absence. What beast couldst thou be, that

373 were not subject to a beast? and what a beast art

374 thou already, that seest not thy loss in

Thy . . . transformation: "what you would lose by being changed to an animal" (Riverside, 1,515)

375 transformation!

APEMANTUS

376 If thou couldst please me with speaking to me, thou

If . . . here: "if it were possible for anything you say to please me, what you've just said (comparing men with beasts) would be pleasing" (Bevington)

377 mightst have hit upon it here: the commonwealth of

378 Athens is become a forest of beasts.

TIMON

379 How has the ass broke the wall, that thou art out of the city?

How: "an interjection introducing a question" (Mowat, 146)

APEMANTUS

380 Yonder comes a poet and a painter: the plague of **Yonder ... painter**:
"Their entry is long
postponed; probably
Shakespeare had second
thoughts but neglected
to delete this line."
(Riverside, 1.516)

381 company light upon thee! I will fear to catch it

382 and give way: when I know not what else to do, I'll **Give way**: "i.e., get out of
the **way**" (Mowat, 146)

383 see thee again.

TIMON

384 When there is nothing living but thee, thou shalt be

385 welcome. I had rather be a beggar's dog than Apemantus.

APEMANTUS

386 Thou art the cap of all the fools alive. **Cap**: "chief" (Riverside,
1,516)

TIMON

387 Would thou wert clean enough to spit upon!

APEMANTUS

388 A plague on thee! thou art too bad to curse.

TIMON

389 All villains that do stand by thee are pure. **By**: "in comparison
with" (Mowat, 146); **are
pure**: "i.e. seem pure by
contrast" (Riverside, 1,516

APEMANTUS

390 There is no leprosy but what thou speak'st.

TIMON

391 If I name thee.

392 I'll beat thee, but I should infect my hands. **I'll**: "i.e., I would"
(Mowat, 146)

APEMANTUS

393 I would my tongue could rot them off!

TIMON

394 Away, thou issue of a mangy dog!

Issue: "offspring" (Wright, 76)

395 Choler does kill me that thou art alive;

Choler: "anger" (Wright, 76)

396 I swound to see thee.

Swound: "swoon" (Riverside, 1,516)

APEMANTUS

397 Would thou wouldst burst!

TIMON

398 Away,

399 Thou tedious rogue! I am sorry I shall lose

400 A stone by thee.

Throws a stone at him

APEMANTUS

401 Beast!

TIMON

402 Slave!

APEMANTUS

403 Toad!

TIMON

404 Rogue, rogue, rogue!

405 I am sick of this false world, and will love nought

406 But even the mere necessities upon 't.

Even: "only"; **mere**: "bare" (Riverside, 1,516); **necessities**: "(of which death is the chief: see next line)" (Hinman, 106)

407 Then, Timon, presently prepare thy grave;

Presently: "without delay" (Riverside, 1,516)

408 Lie where the light foam the sea may beat

409 Thy grave-stone daily: make thine epitaph,

410 That death in me at others' lives may laugh.

That: "in order that"; **in**: "through" (Bevington); **in me**: "by my example" (Charney, 123)

To the gold

411 O thou sweet king-killer, and dear divorce

Dear: "used intensively" (Williams, 75)

412 'Twixt natural son and sire! thou bright defiler

Natural: "i.e. bound by ties of nature" (Riverside, 1,516)

413 Of Hymen's purest bed! thou valiant Mars!

Hymen: "god of marriage"; **Mars**: "alluding to Mars' adultery with Venus" (Riverside, 1,516); "the Roman god of war" (Mowat, 148)

414 Thou ever young, fresh, loved and delicate wooer,

415 Whose blush doth thaw the consecrated snow

Whose . . . lap: "i.e. whose glow overpowers the most steadfast chastity" (Riverside, 1,516)

416 That lies on Dian's lap! thou visible god,

Dian's: "Diana is the Roman goddess of chastity" (Mowat, 148)

417 That solder'st close impossibilities,

Solder'st close: "i.e., solders together, unites" (Mowat, 148); **impossibilities**: "things (otherwise) incapable of being brought together" (Riverside, 1,516)

418 And makest them kiss! that speak'st with

419 every tongue,

420 To every purpose! O thou touch of hearts!

Touch: "touchstone" (Riverside, 1,516)

421 Think, thy slave man rebels, and by thy virtue

Virtue: "power" (Riverside, 1,516)

422 Set them into confounding odds, that beasts

Them: "i.e. men"; **into confounding odds**: "at strife that will destroy them" (Riverside, 1,516); **that**: "i.e., so **that**" (Mowat, 148)

423 May have the world in empire!

APEMANTUS

424 Would 'twere so!

425 But not till I am dead. I'll say thou'st gold:

Thou'st: "thou hast" (Bevington)

426 Thou wilt be throng'd to shortly.

TIMON

427 Throng'd to!

APEMANTUS

428 Ay.

TIMON

429 Thy back, I prithee.

Thy back: "i.e., show me your back" (Bevington)

APEMANTUS

430 Live, and love thy misery.

TIMON

431 Long live so, and so die.

Exit APEMANTUS

432 I am quit.

> **Quit**: "rid (of you)" (Riverside, 1,516)

433 Moe things like men! Eat, Timon, and abhor them.

> **Moe**: "(here come) more. Many editors follow Hanmer in giving this line to Timon." (Riverside, 1,516); **abhor**: "shrink from in disgust" (Wright, 78); **them**: "i.e., the bandits" (Bevington)

Enter Banditti

> ***Banditti***: "bandits, thieves" (Mowat, 148)

FIRST BANDIT

434 Where should he have this gold? It is some poor

> **Where . . . have**: "where can he have got" (Riverside, 1,516)

435 fragment, some slender ort of his remainder: the

> **Ort**: "scrap" (Riverside, 1,516)

436 mere want of gold, and the falling-from of his

> **Mere**: "utter" (Riverside, 1,516); **want**: "lack"; **falling-from**: "i.e., desertion, defection" (Mowat, 150)

437 friends, drove him into this melancholy.

SECOND BANDIT

438 It is noised he hath a mass of treasure.

> **Noised**: "rumored" (Wright, 78)

THIRD BANDIT

439 Let us make the assay upon him: if he care not

Assay: "trial (used to determine the amount of precious metal in ore or alloy)" (Riverside, 1,516)

440 for't, he will supply us easily; if he covetously

For't: "i.e., **for** his gold" (Mowat, 150)

441 reserve it, how shall's get it?

Shall's: "i.e., **shall** we" (Mowat, 150)

SECOND BANDIT

442 True; for he bears it not about him, 'tis hid.

FIRST BANDIT

443 Is not this he?

BANDITTI

444 Where?

SECOND BANDIT

445 'Tis his description.

THIRD BANDIT

446 He; I know him.

ALL BANDITTI

447 'Save thee, Timon.

'Save: "God save" (Riverside, 1,516)

TIMON

448 Now, thieves?

Now: "how now" (Williams, 76)

BANDITTI

449 Soldiers, not thieves.

TIMON

450 Both too; and women's sons.

Both too: "both" (Bevington) **and women's sons**: "i.e., as certainly as your were born of women" (Wright, 78)

BANDITTI

451 We are not thieves, but men that much do want.

> **Want**: "lack. Timon plays on the word in his reply: 'Your greatest feeling of lack is occasioned by the fact that you desire a great deal to eat.'" (Riverside, 1,516)

TIMON

452 Your greatest want is, you want much of meat.

> **Your . . . meat**: "i.e., your greatest deficiency is that you crave such rich food (as Timon goes on to explain)" (Bevington)

453 Why should you want? Behold, the earth hath roots;

454 Within this mile break forth a hundred springs;

455 The oaks bear mast, the briers scarlet hips;

> **Mast**: "acorns, beech nuts, and other fruits of forest trees"; **hips**: "fruit of the wild rose" (Riverside, 1,516)

456 The bounteous huswife, nature, on each bush

> **Huswife**: "housewife (pronounced 'hussif')" (Mowat, 150)

457 Lays her full mess before you. Want! why want?

> **Mess**: "meal" (Riverside, 1,516)

FIRST BANDIT

458 We cannot live on grass, on berries, water,

459 As beasts and birds and fishes.

TIMON

460 Nor on the beasts themselves, the birds, and fishes;

461 You must eat men. Yet thanks I must you con

Thanks ... con: "I must thank you; **con** here means 'acknowledge'" (Wright, 79)

462 That you are thieves profess'd, that you work not

463 In holier shapes: for there is boundless theft

Holier shapes: "more respectable guises" (Riverside, 1,516)

464 In limited professions. Rascal thieves,

Limited: "restricted, officially regulated" (Riverside, 1,516)

465 Here's gold. Go, suck the subtle blood o' the grape,

Subtle: "(1) delicate; (2) insidiously treacherous" (Mowat, 152)

466 Till the high fever seethe your blood to froth,

High fever: "(induced by intoxication)" (Bevington); **seethe**: "boil" (Mowat, 152)

467 And so scape hanging: trust not the physician;

Scape hanging: "i.e. by dying of drink" (Riverside, 1,516)

468 His antidotes are poison, and he slays

469 Moe than you rob: take wealth and lives together;

Moe: "more" (Charney, 126); **take ... together**: "i.e., murder your robbery victims" (Bevington)

470 Do villany, do, since you protest to do't,

Protest: "profess" (Riverside, 1,516)

471 Like workmen. I'll example you with thievery.

Like ... thievery: "i.e. as one does in instructing practitioners of any craft, I'll furnish you with instances of your profession, thievery" (Riverside, 1,517)

472 The sun's a thief, and with his great attraction

Attraction: "drawing power" (Mowat, 152)

473 Robs the vast sea: the moon's an arrant thief,

Arrant: "common, notorious" (Mowat, 152)

474 And her pale fire she snatches from the sun:

475 The sea's a thief, whose liquid surge resolves

The sea's . . . tears: "the image of **the sea** dissolving **the moon into salt tears** draws on the moon's control of the tides" (Mowat, 152); **resolves**: "dissolves" (Riverside, 1,517)

476 The moon into salt tears: the earth's a thief,

The moon: "considered a moist star, not only controller of the ocean's tides but the source of its water" (Wright, 79)

477 That feeds and breeds by a composture stolen

Composture: "compost, manure" (Riverside, 1,517)

478 From general excrement: each thing's a thief:

479 The laws, your curb and whip, in their rough power

480 Has uncheck'd theft. Love not yourselves: away,

Has uncheck'd theft: "i.e., have unrestrained power to steal" (Mowat, 152)

481 Rob one another. There's more gold. Cut throats:

482 All that you meet are thieves: to Athens go,

483 Break open shops; nothing can you steal,

484 But thieves do lose it: steal no less for this

Steal . . . howso'er: "if you steal less because of the gold I am giving you, may gold destroy you whatever happens" (Riverside, 1,517); **for**: "because you have" (Hinman, 109)

485 I give you; and gold confound you howsoe'er!

Amen. **Confound**: "destroy"; **howsoe'er**: "in any case" (Mowat, 152)

THIRD BANDIT

486 Has almost charmed me from my profession, by

Has: "i.e., he **has**" (Mowat, 152)

487 persuading me to it.

FIRST BANDIT

488 'Tis in the malice of mankind that he thus advises

The malice: "i.e. his hatred" (Riverside, 1,517)

489 us; not to have us thrive in our mystery.

Mystery: "trade, craft" (Riverside, 1,517)

SECOND BANDIT

490 I'll believe him as an enemy, and give over my
trade.

I'll . . . enemy: "i.e., since he is an enemy, I'll do the opposite of what he advises"; **give over**: "give up" (Charney,127)

FIRST BANDIT

491 Let us first see peace in Athens: there is no time

Let . . . peace: "let us wait until the war is over (and prospects for stealing are less good)" (Riverside, 1,517)

492 so miserable but a man may be true.

True: "honest" (Riverside, 1,517)

Exeunt Banditti

Enter FLAVIUS

FLAVIUS

493 O you gods!

494 Is yond despised and ruinous man my lord?

Ruinous: "in ruins" (Riverside, 1,517)

495 Full of decay and failing? O monument

Failing: "weakness; failure" (Mowat, 154); **monument / And wonder**: "wonderful monument, awesome memorial" (Riverside, 1,517)

496 And wonder of good deeds evilly bestow'd!

Evilly bestow'd: "wrongly bestowed on the wicked" (Bevington)

497 What an alteration of honor

Alteration of honor: "change (for the worse) in honor" (Charney, 127)

498 Has desperate want made!

499 What vilder thing upon the earth than friends

Vilder: "viler" (Charney, 127)

500 Who can bring noblest minds to basest ends!

501 How rarely does it meet with this time's guise,

How . . . enemies: "i.e. how excellently (*rarely*) does the command to love our enemies suit the fashion of this age" (Riverside, 1,517); **guise**: "fashion, style" (Mowat, 154)

502 When man was wish'd to love his enemies!

Wish'd: "entreated, commanded" (Mowat, 154)

503 Grant I may ever love, and rather woo

504 Those that would mischief me than those that do! **Those ... do**: "those who frankly intend my harm rather than those who harm me (while falsely professing friendship)" (Riverside, 1,517)

505 Has caught me in his eye: I will present **Caught ... eye**: "seen me" (Bevington)

506 My honest grief unto him; and, as my lord,

507 Still serve him with my life. My dearest master!

TIMON

508 Away! what art thou?

FLAVIUS

509 Have you forgot me, sir?

TIMON

510 Why dost ask that? I have forgot all men;

511 Then, if thou grant'st thou'rt a man, I have forgot thee.

FLAVIUS

512 An honest poor servant of yours.

TIMON

513 Then I know thee not:

514 I never had honest man about me, I; all

515 I kept were knaves, to serve in meat to villains. **Knaves**: "(1) servants (2) villains" (Charney, 128); **serve in**: "serve" (Riverside, 1,517)

FLAVIUS

516 The gods are witness,

517 Ne'er did poor steward wear a truer grief

518 For his undone lord than mine eyes for you. **Undone**: "ruined" (Mowat, 154)

TIMON

519 What, dost thou weep? Come nearer. Then I

520 love thee,

521 Because thou art a woman, and disclaim'st

522 Flinty mankind; whose eyes do never give

Flinty: "hardhearted" (Bevington); **give**: "yield tears" (Riverside, 1,517)

523 But thorough lust and laughter. Pity's sleeping:

Thorough: "through, i.e., as a consequence of" (Mowat, 154)

524 Strange times, that weep with laughing, not with weeping!

FLAVIUS

525 I beg of you to know me, good my lord,

526 To accept my grief and whilst this poor wealth lasts

527 To entertain me as your steward still.

Entertain: "employ" (Riverside, 1,517)

TIMON

528 Had I a steward

529 So true, so just, and now so comfortable?

Comfortable: "comforting" (Riverside, 1,517)

530 It almost turns my dangerous nature wild.

Dangerous: "savage" (Bevington); **wild**: "insane. Most editors read *mild*, following Hanmer." (Riverside, 1,517)

531 Let me behold thy face. Surely, this man

532 Was born of woman.

533 Forgive my general and exceptless rashness,

Exceptless: "making no exception" (Riverside, 1,517)

534 You perpetual-sober gods! I do proclaim

Perpetual-sober: "eternally grave and sedate" (Bevington)

535 One honest man--mistake me not--but one;

536 No more, I pray--and he's a steward.

537 How fain would I have hated all mankind!

Fain: "gladly" (Riverside, 1,517)

538 And thou redeem'st thyself: but all, save thee,

And . . . thyself: "but you deliver yourself (from the all-embracing hatred intended)" (Riverside, 1,517)

539 I fell with curses.

Fell: "strike down" (Riverside, 1,517)

540 Methinks thou art more honest now than wise;

Methinks: "it seems to me" (Mowat, 156)

541 For, by oppressing and betraying me,

Oppressing: "distressing" (Charney, 128)

542 Thou mightst have sooner got another service:

Service: "position as a servant" (Charney, 129)

543 For many so arrive at second masters,

544 Upon their first lord's neck. But tell me true—

Upon . . . neck: "i.e. by treading down their first employer" (Riverside, 1,517); **true**: "i.e., truly" (Mowat, 156)

545 For I must ever doubt, though ne'er so sure—

Doubt: "suspect, fear" (Charney, 129)

546 Is not thy kindness subtle, covetous,

Subtle: "artfully contrived" (Mowat, 156)

547 If not a usuring kindness, and, as rich men deal

gifts, **If not**: "These words are usually, and perhaps rightly, omitted by editors, following Pope." (Riverside, 1,517); **deal**: "bestow" (Mowat, 156); **usurping**: "seeking profit" (Wright, 82); **as**: "as what we have when" (Hinman, 111)

548 Expecting in return twenty for one?

FLAVIUS

549 No, my most worthy master; in whose breast

550 Doubt and suspect, alas, are placed too late:

Suspect: "suspicion" (Riverside, 1,517)

551 You should have fear'd false times when you did feast:

552 Suspect still comes where an estate is least.

Still: "always" (Mowat, 156)

553 That which I show, heaven knows, is merely love,

Merely: "purely" (Riverside, 1,517)

554 Duty and zeal to your unmatched mind,

Unmatched: "matchless" (Williams, 80)

555 Care of your food and living; and, believe it,

Care of: "concern for, attention to"; **living**: "livelihood, maintenance" (Mowat, 158)

556 My most honor'd lord,

557 For any benefit that points to me,

For: "i.e., as for"; **points to**: "i.e., is directed toward" (Mowat, 158); **points**: "might accrue" (Charney, 129)

558 Either in hope or present, I'ld exchange

In hope: "i.e., in the future"; **present**: "the present time" (Mowat, 158)

559 For this one wish, that you had power and wealth

560 To requite me, by making rich yourself.

Requite: "repay"
(Mowat, 158)

TIMON

561 Look thee, 'tis so! Thou singly honest man,

Singly: "(1) uniquely; (2) sincerely" (Riverside, 1,517)

562 Here, take: the gods out of my misery

563 Has sent thee treasure. Go, live rich and happy;

Has: "i.e., have"
(Mowat, 158)

564 But thus condition'd: thou shalt build from men;

Thus condition'd: "on these conditions"; **from**: "remote from" (Riverside, 1,517)

565 Hate all, curse all, show charity to none,

566 But let the famish'd flesh slide from the bone,

567 Ere thou relieve the beggar; give to dogs

568 What thou deny'st to men; let prisons swallow 'em,

569 Debts wither 'em to nothing; be men like

Be men: "i.e., let **men be**" (Mowat, 158)

570 blasted woods,

Blasted: "blighted, withered" (Riverside, 1,518)

571 And may diseases lick up their false bloods!

572 And so farewell and thrive.

FLAVIUS

573 O, let me stay,

574 And comfort you, my master.

TIMON

575 If thou hatest curses,

576 Stay not; fly, whilst thou art blest and free:

577 Ne'er see thou man, and let me ne'er see thee.

Exit FLAVIUS. TIMON retires to his cave

ACT V

SCENE I. The woods. Before Timon's cave.

Enter Poet and Painter; TIMON watching them from his cave

PAINTER

1 As I took note of the place, it cannot be far where

2 he abides.

POET

3 What's to be thought of him? does the rumor hold   **Hold / for**: "prove"
  (Williams, 81)

4 for true, that he's so full of gold?

PAINTER

5 Certain: Alcibiades reports it; Phrynia and

6 Timandra had gold of him: he likewise enriched poor

7 straggling soldiers with great quantity: 'tis said   **Soldiers**: "The Banditti
  claimed to be **soldiers** at
  4.3.449." (Mowat, 162)

8 he gave unto his steward a mighty sum.

POET

9 Then this breaking of his has been but a try for his   friends. **Breaking**:
  "bankruptcy"; **try**: "test"
  (Riverside, 1,518)

PAINTER

10 Nothing else: you shall see him a palm in Athens

> **Palm**: "perhaps an allusion to Psalm 92.12: 'The righteous shall **flourish** like a **palm** tree.'" (Mowat, 162); "lofty figure; great man" (Wright, 84)

11 again, and flourish with the highest. Therefore

12 'tis not amiss we tender our loves to him, in this

> **Tender**: "offer" (Mowat, 162)

13 supposed distress of his: it will show honestly in

> **Show honestly**: "appear honorable" (Riverside, 1,518)

14 us; and is very likely to load our purposes with

> **Load**: "reward" (Riverside, 1,518); **purposes**: "plans" (Williams, 82)

15 what they travail for, if it be a just true report

> **Travail**: "(1) labor; (2) travel (The words *travial* and *travel* were not distinguished from each other.)" (Mowat, 162)

16 that goes of his having.

> **Goes of his having**: "is current about his wealth" (Bevington)

POET

17 What have you now to present unto him?

PAINTER

18 Nothing at this time but my visitation: only I will

> **Visitation**: "visit. Shakespeare knew the word *visit* only as a verb" (Riverside, 1,518)

19 promise him an excellent piece.

POET

20 I must serve him so too, tell him of an intent

Intent: "project, design" (Mowat, 162)

21 that's coming toward him.

Coming toward: "intended for" (Bevington)

PAINTER

22 Good as the best. Promising is the very air o' the

Good as the best: "excellent" (Wright, 85); **air**: "manner, style" (Mowat, 164)

23 time: it opens the eyes of expectation:

Opens the eyes of: "arouses" (Wright, 85)

24 performance is ever the duller for his act; and,

His act: "its performance" (Riverside, 1,518)

25 but in the plainer and simpler kind of people, the

But in: "i.e., except with" (Mowat, 164)

26 deed of saying is quite out of use. To promise is

Deed of saying: "fulfillment of promise" (Riverside, 1,518); **use**: "practice, custom" (Mowat, 164)

27 most courtly and fashionable: performance is a kind

28 of will or testament which argues a great sickness

29 in his judgment that makes it.

TIMON comes from his cave, behind

TIMON

30 [Aside] Excellent workman! thou canst not paint a

31 man so bad as is thyself.

POET

32 I am thinking what I shall say I have provided for

Provided: "arranged" (Mowat, 164)

33 him: it must be a personating of himself; a satire **Personating of himself**: "representation of Timon and his situation" (Charney, 132)

34 against the softness of prosperity, with a discovery **Softness**: "comfort; luxury; easy or voluptuous living" (Mowat, 164); **discovery**: "exposure" (Riverside, 1,518)

35 of the infinite flatteries that follow youth and opulency.

TIMON

36 [Aside] Must thou needs stand for a villain in **Must thou needs**: "i.e., must you" (Mowat, 164); **stand**: "be a model" (Riverside, 1,518)

37 thine own work? wilt thou whip thine own faults in **Whip . . . men**: "proverbial" (Wright, 85)

38 other men? Do so, I have gold for thee.

POET

39 Nay, let's seek him:

40 Then do we sin against our own estate, **Estate**: "material prosperity" (Mowat, 164)

41 When we may profit meet, and come too late.

PAINTER

42 True;

43 When the day serves, before black-corner'd night, **Serves**: "is available" (Mowat, 164); **black-corner'd**: "obscuring things as in dark corners" (Riverside, 1,518)

44 Find what thou want'st by free and offer'd light. Come. **Free and offer'd light**: "the light of day, freely offered to all" (Bevington)

TIMON

45 [Aside] I'll meet you at the turn. What a
      Meet . . . turn: "Obscure; perhaps 'play you at your own game' (Maxwell)." (Riverside, 1,518)

46 god's gold,

47 That he is worshipp'd in a baser temple
      Temple: "the human body" (Wright, 86)

48 Than where swine feed!

49 'Tis thou that rigg'st the bark and plough'st the foam,
      Thou: "i.e., **gold**"; **rigg'st . . . foam**: "i.e., cause men to rig ships and sail the seas (by providing the motivation for exploration and colonization)" (Mowat, 164)

50 Settlest admired reverence in a slave:
      Settlest . . . slave: "causes a slave to admire and venerate his master" (Riverside, 1,518)

51 To thee be worship! and thy saints for aye
      Worship: "devout respect" (Wright, 86); **thy saints**: "may your saints" (Bevington); **aye**: "ever" (Mowat, 164)

52 Be crown'd with plagues that thee alone obey!
      Be: "i.e., may they be" (Charney, 133)

53 Fit I meet them.
      Fit: "perhaps, it is fitting that" (Mowat, 164)

Coming forward

POET

54 Hail, worthy Timon!

PAINTER

55 Our late noble master!

Late: "recently, not long since" (Mowat, 166)

TIMON

56 Have I once lived to see two honest men?

Once: "actually, indeed" (Riverside, 1,518)

POET

57 Sir,

58 Having often of your open bounty tasted,

Open: "liberal, generous" (Mowat, 166)

59 Hearing you were retired, your friends fall'n off,

Retired: "withdrawn into seclusion"; **fall'n off**: "i.e., having deserted you" (Mowat, 166)

60 Whose thankless natures--O abhorred spirits!--

61 Not all the whips of heaven are large enough:

62 What! to you,

63 Whose star-like nobleness gave life and influence

Influence: "i.e. astral influence" (Riverside, 1,519)

64 To their whole being! I am rapt and cannot cover

Rapt: "carried out of myself, at a loss for words" (Riverside, 1,518)

65 The monstrous bulk of this ingratitude

66 With any size of words.

Size: "(1) magnitude (2) starch-like glue used on cloth, especially before painting on it" (Charney, 133); **size of**: "i.e. adequate" (Hinman, 114)

TIMON

67 Let it go naked, men may see't the better:

Let it go naked: "reflecting the proverb 'Truth shows best being naked.'" (Wright, 86)

68 You that are honest, by being what you are,

69 Make them best seen and known.

Them: "i.e. ungrateful men" (Riverside, 1,518)

PAINTER

70 He and myself

71 Have travail'd in the great shower of your gifts,

Travail'd: "(1) traveled; (2) exerted ourselves" (Wright, 86)

72 And sweetly felt it.

TIMON

73 Ay, you are honest men.

PAINTER

74 We are hither come to offer you our service.

TIMON

75 Most honest men! Why, how shall I requite you?

Requite: "repay" (Mowat, 166)

76 Can you eat roots, and drink cold water? no.

BOTH

77 What we can do, we'll do, to do you service.

TIMON

78 Ye're honest men: ye've heard that I have gold;

79 I am sure you have: speak truth; ye're honest men.

PAINTER

80 So it is said, my noble lord; but therefore

Therefore . . . I: "it was not for that reason that we came" (Riverside, 1,519)

81 Came not my friend nor I.

TIMON

82 Good honest men! Thou draw'st a counterfeit

Counterfeit: "portrait (but Timon intends also the fraudulent sense)" (Riverside,1,519)

83 Best in all Athens: thou'rt, indeed, the best;

84 Thou counterfeit'st most lively.

Thou . . . lively: "(1) you paint very realistically; (2) you are a living counterfeit" (Riverside, 1,519); **lively**: "vividly" (Mowat, 168)

PAINTER

85 So, so, my lord.

So, so: "passably" (Riverside, 1,519)

TIMON

86 E'en so, sir, as I say. And, for thy fiction,

And for: "i.e., **and as for**" (Mowat, 168); **fiction, swells, stuff, smooth**: "These are all words capable of being taken in two ways." (Riverside, 1,519); **fiction**: "imaginative feigning" (Charney, 134)

87 Why, thy verse swells with stuff so fine and smooth

Swells . . . smooth: "(1) is elegantly styled and adorned (2) is a vainglorious concoction of specious fabrication" (Bevington)

88 That thou art even natural in thine art.

Thou . . . art: "(1) your art equals nature; (2) the feigning of your art reveals your own nature" (Riverside, 1,519); **natural**: "pun on 'natural,' a fool" (Williams, 84)

89 But, for all this, my honest-natured friends,

90 I must needs say you have a little fault:

91 Marry, 'tis not monstrous in you, neither wish I

Marry: "indeed" (Charney, 134); **monstrous**: "unnatural" (Bevington)

92 You take much pains to mend.

Mend: "rectify, remove" (Mowat, 168)

BOTH

93 Beseech your honor

Beseech: "i.e., we beseech" (Mowat, 168)

94 To make it known to us.

TIMON

95 You'll take it ill.

Ill: "badly" (Mowat, 168)

BOTH

96 Most thankfully, my lord.

TIMON

97 Will you, indeed?

BOTH

98 Doubt it not, worthy lord.

TIMON

99 There's never a one of you but trusts a knave,

There's ... but: "i.e., each of you" (Bevington)

100 That mightily deceives you.

BOTH

101 Do we, my lord?

TIMON

102 Ay, and you hear him cog, see him dissemble,

Cog: "cheat" (Riverside, 1,519)

103 Know his gross patchery, love him, feed him,

Patchery: "knavery" (Riverside, 1,519)

213

104 Keep in your bosom: yet remain assured	**Keep**: "i.e., **keep** him" (Mowat, 168)
105 That he's a made-up villain.	**Made-up**: "complete" (Riverside, 1,519)

PAINTER

106 I know none such, my lord.

POET

107 Nor I.

TIMON

108 Look you, I love you well; I'll give you gold,

109 Rid me these villains from your companies:	**Rid me**: "i.e., if you will **rid**" (Mowat, 168)
110 Hang them or stab them, drown them in a draught,	**Draught**: "privy" (Riverside, 1,519)
111 Confound them by some course, and come to me,	**Confound**: "get rid of" (Riverside, 1,519); **course**: "means" (Bevington)

112 I'll give you gold enough.

BOTH

113 Name them, my lord, let's know them.	**Let's**: let us

TIMON

114 You that way and you this, but two in company;	**Two in company**: "i.e. each still in company with another" (Riverside, 1,519)

115 Each man apart, all single and alone,

116 Yet an arch-villain keeps him company.

117 If where thou art two villains shall not be,	**Shall not**: "are not to" (Riverside, 1,519)
118 Come not near him. If thou wouldst not reside	**Him**: "i.e., the other one" (Bevington)
119 But where one villain is, then him abandon.	**But**: "except" (Charney, 135)

120 Hence, pack! there's gold; you came for gold, ye slaves:

Pack: "be off" (Riverside, 1,519)

To Painter

121 You have work for me; there's payment for you: hence!

Work: "i.e., a **work** or poem" (Mowat, 170); **there's payment**: "i.e., here's a beating or a thrown stone" (Bevington)

To Poet

122 You are an alcumist; make gold of that.

Alcumist: "alchemist"; **that**: "probably a thrown stone; another may have been the 'payment' of line 121." (Riverside, 1,519)

123 Out, rascal dogs!

Beats them out, and then retires to his cave

Enter FLAVIUS and two Senators

FLAVIUS

124 It is in vain that you would speak with Timon;

125 For he is set so only to himself

Set . . . to: "so completely intent upon" (Riverside, 1,519)

126 That nothing but himself which looks like man

127 Is friendly with him.

Friendly with: "congenial to" (Riverside, 1,519)

FIRST SENATOR

128 Bring us to his cave:

129 It is our part and promise to the Athenians

Our . . . Athenians: "i.e. the part we have promised the Athenians we will play" (Riverside, 1,519); **part**: "function, duty, business" (Mowat, 170)

130 To speak with Timon.

SECOND SENATOR

131 At all times alike

132 Men are not still the same: 'twas time and griefs | **Still the same**: "synonymous with *At all times alike*"; **griefs**: "grievances" (Riverside, 1,519)

133 That fram'd him thus: time, with his fairer hand, | **Fram'd**: "shaped, i.e. altered" (Riverside, 1,519); **with his**: "i.e., **with** its" (Mowat, 170)

134 Offering the fortunes of his former days,

135 The former man may make him. Bring us to him, | **The former . . . him**: "may turn him into his former self" (Bevington)

136 And chance it as it may. | **Chance it**: "let it turn out" (Riverside, 1,519)

FLAVIUS

137 Here is his cave.

138 Peace and content be here! Lord Timon! Timon!

139 Look out, and speak to friends: the Athenians,

140 By two of their most reverend senate, greet thee: | **Reverend**: "honored" (Wright, 89)

141 Speak to them, noble Timon.

TIMON comes from his cave

TIMON

142 Thou sun, that comfort'st, burn! Speak, and

143 be hang'd:

144 For each true word, a blister! and each false | **A blister**: "proverbially, lies were supposed to blister the tongue" (Wright, 89)

216

145 Be as cantherizing to the root o' the tongue,

Cantherizing: "most editors substitute *Cauterizing*" (Riverside, 1,519); searing with acid or a hot iron" (Hinman, 117)

146 Consuming it with speaking!

FIRST SENATOR

147 Worthy Timon--

TIMON

148 Of none but such as you, and you of Timon.

Of . . . Timon: "i.e., we are worthy of nothing better than being punished by one another" (Bevington)

FIRST SENATOR

149 The senators of Athens greet thee, Timon.

TIMON

150 I thank them; and would send them back the plague,

151 Could I but catch it for them.

FIRST SENATOR

152 O, forget

153 What we are sorry for ourselves in thee.

What . . . thee: "those wrongs that we regret having done you" (Bevington)

154 The senators with one consent of love

One . . . love: "a single loving voice" (Riverside, 1,519); **consent**: "agreement" (Wright, 90)

155 Entreat thee back to Athens; who have thought

156 On special dignities, which vacant lie

157 For thy best use and wearing.

Thy best use: "use by thee, whom best they fit" (Wright, 90)

SECOND SENATOR

158 They confess

159 Toward thee forgetfulness too general gross:

General gross: "obvious to everybody" (Riverside, 1,519)

160 Which now the public body, which doth seldom

Public body: "perhaps, Athens, or, perhaps, the senate of Athens" (Mowat, 172)

161 Play the recanter, feeling in itself

Play the recanter: "i.e., changes its mind and apologize" (Bevington)

162 A lack of Timon's aid, hath sense withal

Timon's aid: "aid to Timon. (But suggesting also 'aid to be given by Timon to Athens.')" (Bevington); **hath sense withal**: "becomes aware at the same time" (Riverside, 1,519); **withal**: "because of that, or as a consequence of that" (Mowat, 172)

163 Of it own fall, restraining aid to Timon;

It: "its"; **fall**: "decline, defection from virtue"; **restraining**: "in holding back" (Riverside, 1,519)

164 And send forth us, to make their sorrowed render,

Sorrowed render: "sorrowful acknowledgment" (Riverside, 1,520)

165 Together with a recompense more fruitful

Fruitful: "abundant" (Riverside, 1,520)

166 Than their offence can weigh down by the dram; **Weigh . . . dram**: "outweigh even if measured out to the last fraction of an ounce" (Riverside, 1,520)

167 Ay, even such heaps and sums of love and wealth

168 As shall to thee blot out what wrongs were theirs **Theirs**: "of their doing" (Riverside, 1,520)

169 And write in thee the figures of their love, **Figures**: "(1) shapes, signs; (2) amounts"; **of their love**: "that show how much they love you" (Riverside, 1,520)

170 Ever to read them thine. **Read them thine**: "read in them how much they are yours" (Wright, 90)

TIMON

171 You witch me in it; **Witch**: "enchant" (Mowat, 172)

172 Surprise me to the very brink of tears: **Surprise**: "overcome" (Riverside, 1,520)

173 Lend me a fool's heart and a woman's eyes,

174 And I'll beweep these comforts, worthy senators. **Beweep these comforts**: "weep over these comforting reflections" (Mowat, 174); **comforts**: "pleasures" (Charney,138)

FIRST SENATOR

175 Therefore, so please thee to return with us **So**: "if it" (Riverside, 1,520)

176 And of our Athens, thine and ours, to take

177 The captainship, thou shalt be met with thanks,

178 Allow'd with absolute power and thy good name **Allow'd**: "endowed" (Riverside, 1,520); sanctioned" (Williams, 87)

179 Live with authority: so soon we shall drive back   **Live**: "i.e., continue to be associated" (Mowat, 174)

180 Of Alcibiades the approaches wild,   **Of . . . wild**: "the savage attacks of Alcibiades" (Bevington)

181 Who, like a boar too savage, doth root up

182 His country's peace.

SECOND SENATOR

183 And shakes his threatening sword

184 Against the walls of Athens.

FIRST SENATOR

185 Therefore, Timon--

TIMON

186 Well, sir, I will; therefore, I will, sir; thus:

187 If Alcibiades kill my countrymen,

188 Let Alcibiades know this of Timon,

189 That Timon cares not. But if he sack fair Athens,

190 And take our goodly aged men by the beards,

191 Giving our holy virgins to the stain   **Stain**: "pollution" (Bevington)

192 Of contumelious, beastly, mad-brain'd war,   **Contumelious**: "insolent" (Riverside, 1,520)

193 Then let him know, and tell him Timon speaks it,

194 In pity of our aged and our youth,

195 I cannot choose but tell him, that I care not,   **Cannot choose . . . him**: "cannot help telling him" (Wright, 91)

196 And let him take't at worst; for their knives care

> not, **Take't at worst**: "put the worst construction on it" (Riverside, 1,520); **for . . . not**: "don't be concerned about the enemies' knives" (Wright, 91)

197 While you have throats to answer: for myself,

> **Answer**: "be answerable, suffer the consequences" (Riverside, 1,520); **for myself**: "i.e., as **for myself**" (Mowat, 174)

198 There's not a whittle in the unruly camp

> **Whittle**: "clasp-knife"; **unruly**; "rebel" (Riverside, 1,520)

199 But I do prize it at my love before

> **Prize**: "value" (Bevington); **at my love**: "perhaps, in terms of **my love**, or, as worthy of **my love**: "(Mowat, 174); **before**: "above" (Bevington)

200 The reverend'st throat in Athens. So I leave you

> **Reverend'st**: "most venerable" (Wright, 91)

201 To the protection of the prosperous gods,

> **Prosperous**: "propitious" (Riverside, 1,520)

202 As thieves to keepers.

> **Keepers**: "jailers (who 'protect' thieves for the hangman)" (Riverside, 1,520)

FLAVIUS

203 Stay not, all's in vain.

TIMON

204 Why, I was writing of my epitaph;

> **Writing of**: "i.e., **writing**" (Mowat, 174)

205 it will be seen to-morrow: my long sickness

206 Of health and living now begins to mend,

Health and living: "healthful living" (Wright, 91); **mend**: "improve" (Mowat, 176)

207 And nothing brings me all things. Go, live still;

Nothing: "i.e. death" (Riverside, 1,520); "extinction" (Mowat, 176)

208 Be Alcibiades your plague, you his,

209 And last so long enough!

At last . . . enough: "remain in that state as long as possible" (Bevington)

FIRST SENATOR

210 We speak in vain.

TIMON

211 But yet I love my country, and am not

Yet: "still" (Bevington)

212 One that rejoices in the common wrack,

Common wrack: "destruction of the community" (Mowat, 176)

213 As common bruit doth put it.

Bruit: "rumor" (Riverside, 1,520)

FIRST SENATOR

214 That's well spoke.

TIMON

215 Commend me to my loving countrymen—

Commend me to: "give my greetings to" (Wright, 92)

FIRST SENATOR

216 These words become your lips as they pass

Become: "grace, do credit to" (Bevington)

217 thorough them.

Thorough: "through" (Wright, 92)

SECOND SENATOR

218 And enter in our ears like great triumphers

Triumphers: "conquerors, victors" (Mowat, 176)

219 In their applauding gates.

Applauding gates: "i.e., gates crowded with applauding citizens" (Bevington)

TIMON

220 Commend me to them,

221 And tell them that, to ease them of their griefs,

222 Their fears of hostile strokes, their aches, losses,

Aches: "pronounced 'aitchs'" (Mowat, 176)

223 Their pangs of love, with other incident throes

Incident throes: "i.e., agonies that are likely to happen" (Mowat, 176)

224 That nature's fragile vessel doth sustain

Nature's . . . vessel: "i.e., the body" (Bevington)

225 In life's uncertain voyage, I will some kindness do them:

226 I'll teach them to prevent wild Alcibiades' wrath.

Prevent: "frustrate, forestall (with a quibble on 'anticipate')" (Bevington)

FIRST SENATOR

227 I like this well; he will return again.

TIMON

228 I have a tree, which grows here in my close,

In my close: "i.e. alongside my cave" (Hinman, 120); **close**: "enclosure" (Riverside, 1,520); "yard" (Wright, 92)

229 That mine own use invites me to cut down,

Use: "need; advantage" (Mowat, 176)

230 And shortly must I fell it: tell my friends,

Fell: "cut" (Bevington)

231 Tell Athens, in the sequence of degree

Degree: "rank"
(Riverside, 1,520)

232 From high to low throughout, that whoso please

233 To stop affliction, let him take his haste,

Take . . . haste: "make haste" (Williams, 89)

234 Come hither, ere my tree hath felt the axe,

235 And hang himself. I pray you, do my greeting.

FLAVIUS

236 Trouble him no further; thus you still shall find him.

Still: "always" (Mowat, 178)

TIMON

237 Come not to me again: but say to Athens,

238 Timon hath made his everlasting mansion

Everlasting mansion: "i.e., grave" (Bevington)

239 Upon the beached verge of the salt flood;

Beached verge: "beach at the edge" (Riverside, 1,520); **verge**: "margin, i.e., shore"; **salt flood**: "i.e., sea, ocean" (Mowat, 178)

240 Who once a day with his embossed froth

Who: "object of *cover* (line 241); the sense here is probably 'which' (as often) rather than 'whom'"; **embossed**: "foaming" (Riverside, 1,520); **his**: "i.e., its" (Mowat, 178)

241 The turbulent surge shall cover: thither come,

242 And let my grave-stone be your oracle.

Oracle: "i.e. source of wisdom" (Riverside, 1,520)

243 Lips, let four words go by and language end:

Four: "indefinite" (Riverside, 1,520)

244 What is amiss plague and infection mend! | **Mend**: "rectify, put right" (Mowat, 178)

245 Graves only be men's works and death their gain!

246 Sun, hide thy beams! Timon hath done his reign.

Retires to his cave

FIRST SENATOR

247 His discontents are unremovably | **Unremovably**: "irremovably" (Mowat, 178)

248 Coupled to nature. | **Coupled to nature**: "made part of his nature" (Riverside, 1,520)

SECOND SENATOR

249 Our hope in him is dead: let us return,

250 And strain what other means is left unto us | **Strain**: "exert to the limit" (Riverside, 1,520)

251 In our dear peril. | **Dear**: "extreme, dire" (Riverside, 1,520)

FIRST SENATOR

252 It requires swift foot. | **Foot**: "movement" (Mowat, 178)

Exeunt

SCENE II. Before the walls of Athens.

Enter two Senators and a Messenger

FIRST SENATOR

1 Thou hast painfully discover'd: are his files | **Painfully discover'd**: "reconnoitered painstakingly (?) or revealed distressing news (?)" (Riverside, 1,520); **files**: "military ranks" (Bevington)

2 As full as thy report?

MESSENGER

3 I have spoke the least:

> **Spoke the least**: "given the most conservative estimate" (Riverside, 1,520)

4 Besides, his expedition promises

> **Expedition**: "speed" (Riverside, 1,521)

5 Present approach.

> **Present**: "immediate" (Wright, 93)

SECOND SENATOR

6 We stand much hazard, if they bring not Timon.

> **Stand much**: "i.e., remain at great" (Mowat, 180); **they**: "i.e., the senators who were sent to Timon" (Bevington)

MESSENGER

7 I met a courier, one mine ancient friend;

> **Mine ancient friend**: "an old friend of mine" (Wright, 93)

8 Whom, though in general part we were opposed,

> **Whom**: "syntactically superfluous"; **general parts**: "public quarrel" (Riverside, 1,521)

9 Yet our old love made a particular force,

> **Particular**: "personal" (Riverside, 1,521)

10 And made us speak like friends: this man was riding

11 From Alcibiades to Timon's cave,

12 With letters of entreaty, which imported

> **Which imported**: "the import of which was (possibly with some admixture of the sense of *importuned*, 'besought')" (Riverside, 1,521); **imported**: "concerned" (Wright, 94)

13 His fellowship i' the cause against your city,

Fellowship: "cooperation, participation" (Riverside, 1,521)

14 In part for his sake mov'd.

In . . . mov'd: "undertaken partly in his (Timon's) behalf" (Riverside, 1,521); **mov'd**: "stirred up, commenced" (Mowat, 180)

FIRST SENATOR

15 Here come our brothers.

Enter the Senators from TIMON

THIRD SENATOR

16 No talk of Timon, nothing of him expect.

No talk: "i.e., let us not talk" (Charney, 142)

17 The enemies' drum is heard, and fearful scouring

Scouring: "scurrying about" (Riverside, 1,521)

18 Doth choke the air with dust: in, and prepare:

In: "let us go in" (Bevington)

19 Ours is the fall, I fear; our foes the snare.

Ours . . . snare: "our part, I fear, is to fall, our foe's part is to set the trap" (Bevington); **foes**: "Many editors read *foe's* (or *foes'*), perhaps rightly." (Riverside, 1,521)

Exeunt

SCENE III. The woods. Timon's cave, and a rude tomb seen.

Enter a Soldier, seeking TIMON

SOLDIER

1 By all description this should be the place.

2 Who's here? speak, ho! No answer! What is this?

What is this: "(presumably the Soldier finds an inscription or trial epitaph composed by Timon in English, which the Soldier can read, whereas the epitaph on Timon's tomb is in Latin, which the Soldier cannot read)" (Charney, 142)

3 Timon is dead, who hath outstretch'd his span:

Outstrech'd his span: "reached the utmost limit of his allotted time" (Riverside, 1,521)

4 Some beast rear'd this; there does not live a man.

There . . . man: "i.e. all men are beasts" (Riverside, 1,521)

5 Dead, sure; and this his grave. What's on this tomb

6 I cannot read; the character I'll take with wax:

Cannot read: "(apparently because in a strange language, as a Latin epitaph would be to an Elizabethan soldier)" (Hinman, 122); **the character . . . wax**: "i.e., **I'll take** a **wax** impression of the **character** (inscription)" (Mowat, 180); **character**: "writing" (Williams, 91)

7 Our captain hath in every figure skill,

Hath . . . skill: "has knowledge of every kind of language" (Wright, 94); **figure**: "written character" (Charney, 142)

8 An ag'd interpreter, though young in days:

Ag'd: "i.e. experienced" (Riverside, 1,521)

9 Before proud Athens he's set down by this,

Set down: "encampled";
by this: "i.e., by now"
(Mowat, 182)

10 Whose fall the mark of his ambition is.

Whose fall: "the fall
of which" (Bevington)
mark: "goal" (Riverside,
1,521)

Exit

SCENE IV. Before the walls of Athens.

Trumpets sound. Enter ALCIBIADES with his powers

Powers: "army"
(Mowat, 182)

ALCIBIADES

1 Sound to this coward and lascivious town

Sound: "proclaim"
(Bevington); **coward**;
"i.e., cowardly"
(Mowat, 182)

2 Our terrible approach.

Terrible: "terrifying"
(Mowat, 182)

A parley sounded

Parley: "a trumpet call
to initiate discussion
between representatives
of opposed forces"
(Mowat, 182)

Enter Senators on the walls

On the walls: "i.e.,
upon the upper stage"
(Charney, 143)

3 Till now you have gone on and fill'd the time
4 With all licentious measure, making your wills

All licentious measure:
"the utmost degree of
license" (Riverside, 1,521);
making . . . justice: "i.e.,
reducing **justice** to the
attainment of your desires"
(Mowat, 182)

5 The scope of justice; till now myself and such **Scope**: "measure" (Riverside, 1,521)

6 As slept within the shadow of your power **Slept**: "i.e., dwelled" (Bevington); (1) were asleep, inactive (2) lived" (Charney, 143)

7 Have wander'd with our travers'd arms and breath'd **Travers'd arms**: "probably in a military sense, 'small arms held in a non-firing position'; possibly 'folded arms,' signifying dejection" (Riverside, 1,521); **breath'd . . . vainly**: "i.e., spoke of our suffering in vain" (Mowat, 182)

8 Our sufferance vainly: now the time is flush, **Sufferance**: "complaint" (Wright, 95); **flush**: "at flood, i.e. ripe for action" (Riverside, 1,521)

9 When crouching marrow in the bearer strong **When . . . strong**: "i.e., when the resolute man's courage is aroused" (Charney, 143); **crouching**: "(formerly) submissive"; **marrow**: "vital strength" (Riverside, 1,521); **strong**: "strongly" (Wright, 95)

10 Cries of itself "No more:" now breathless wrong **Of itself**: "on its own volition" (Mowat, 182); **breathless wrong**: "wrongdoers breathless with fear" (Riverside, 1,521)

11 Shall sit and pant in your great chairs of ease,

Great chairs of ease: "comfortably upholstered chairs of state" (Charney, 143)

12 And pursy insolence shall break his wind

Pursy insolence: "the short-winded tyrant" (Wright, 95); **break his wind**: "pant for breath (perhaps suggesting also to void air from the bowels in fright)" (Bevington)

13 With fear and horrid flight.

Horrid: "terrified" (Riverside, 1,521); "horrible" (Charney, 143)

FIRST SENATOR

14 Noble and young,

15 When thy first griefs were but a mere conceit,

Griefs: "grievances" (Riverside, 1,521); **a mere conceit**: "i.e., nothing but your own fancies" (Mowat, 182)

16 Ere thou hadst power or we had cause of fear,

17 We sent to thee, to give thy rages balm,

18 To wipe out our ingratitude with loves

19 Above their quantity.

Above their quantity: "i.e. greater than your griefs and rages" (Riverside, 1,521)

SECOND SENATOR

20 So did we woo

21 Transformed Timon to our city's love

22 By humble message and by promised means:

Means: "terms of reconciliation (?) or wealth (?)" (Riverside, 1,521)

23 We were not all unkind, nor all deserve

All: "altogether" (Hinman, 124)

24 The common stroke of war.

Common: "indiscriminate" (Bevington)

FIRST SENATOR

25 These walls of ours

26 Were not erected by their hands from whom

27 You have received your grief; nor are they such

They: "Many editors follow Theobald in emending *grief* to *griefs*, to provide a plural antecedent for *they*. But *they* can refer to those who aggrieved Timon, as *them* in line 30 does." (Riverside, 1,521)

28 That these great towers, trophies and schools

Trophies: "monuments" (Riverside, 1,521); **schools**: "public buildings" (Mowat, 184)

29 should fall

30 For private faults in them.

Them: "i.e., those **from whom / You have received your grief**" (Mowat, 184); **private**: "personal"; **them**: "i.e., those from whom you have received your injuries" (Bevington)

SECOND SENATOR

31 Nor are they living

32 Who were the motives that you first went out;

Motives . . . out: "instigators of your banishment" (Riverside, 1,521)

33 Shame that they wanted cunning, in excess

Shame . . . excess: "Obscure; probably 'shame at finding themselves (unexpectedly) deficient in the extremes of low cunning.'" (Riverside, 1,521)

34 Hath broke their hearts. March, noble lord,

35 Into our city with thy banners spread:

36 By decimation, and a tithed death--

Tithed death: "the killing of one person in ten (synonymous with *decimation*)" (Riverside, 1,521)

37 If thy revenges hunger for that food

That food: "i.e., human blood" (Wright, 96)

38 Which nature loathes--take thou the destined tenth,

39 And by the hazard of the spotted die

Die: "(Singular of *dice*; with a play on the verb *die*.)" (Bevington)

40 Let die the spotted.

Spotted: "guilty" (Riverside, 1,521); "with a pun on 'faulty'" (Wright, 96)

FIRST SENATOR

41 All have not offended;

42 For those that were, it is not square to take

Square: "just" (Riverside, 1,521)

43 On those that are, revenges: crimes, like lands,

Like . . . not: "are not, like lands" (Riverside, 1,521); **are**: "are now alive" (Bevington)

44 Are not inherited. Then, dear countryman,

45 Bring in thy ranks, but leave without thy rage:

Without: "outside" (Riverside, 1,521)

46 Spare thy Athenian cradle and those kin

Thy Athenian cradle: "Athens, your birthplace" (Bevington)

47 Which in the bluster of thy wrath must fall

Bluster: "tempest" (Riverside, 1,522)

48 With those that have offended: like a shepherd,

49 Approach the fold and cull the infected forth,

Fold: "enclosure for sheep or the flock itself" (Charney, 145); **cull . . . forth**: "pick out" (Wright, 97)

50 But kill not all together.

SECOND SENATOR

51 What thou wilt,

52 Thou rather shalt enforce it with thy smile

53 Than hew to't with thy sword.

Hew to't: "cut your way to it" (Wright, 97)

FIRST SENATOR

54 Set but thy foot

55 Against our rampir'd gates, and they shall ope;

Rampir'd: "strengthened against attack, as by ramparts" (Riverside, 1,522); **ope**: "open" (Bevington)

56 So thou wilt send thy gentle heart before,

So: "provided that" (Mowat, 184)

57 To say thou'lt enter friendly.

SECOND SENATOR

58 Throw thy glove,

Throw: "i.e., if you will **throw**" (Mowat, 184)

59 Or any token of thine honor else,

Token: "pledge"
(Bevington)

60 That thou wilt use the wars as thy redress

That thou: "i.e., as a
sign that you"; **redress**:
"i.e., means of **redress** or
reparation" (Mowat, 184)

61 And not as our confusion, all thy powers

Our confusion: "i.e.,
a means for **our** ruin
or destruction"; **all thy
powers**: "your whole
army" (Mowat, 186)

62 Shall make their harbor in our town, till we

Make their harbor: "be
quartered" (Riverside,
1,522)

63 Have seal'd thy full desire.

Seal'd: "irrevocably
ratified" (Mowat, 186)

ALCIBIADES

64 Then there's my glove;

65 Descend, and open your uncharged ports:

Uncharged ports:
"unassailed gates"
(Riverside, 1,522)

66 Those enemies of Timon's and mine own

67 Whom you yourselves shall set out for reproof

Set out: "expose"
(Mowat, 186); **reproof**:
"shame" (Charney, 145)

68 Fall and no more: and, to atone your fears

Atone: "appease"
(Riverside, 1,522)

69 With my more noble meaning, not a man

Meaning: "intention";
man: "i.e. soldier of mine"
(Riverside, 1,522)

70 Shall pass his quarter, or offend the stream

Pass his quarter: "go
beyond his assigned
area" (Riverside, 1,522);
offend . . . justice: "violate
the norms set by established
law" (Bevington)

71 Of regular justice in your city's bounds,

72 But shall be remedied to your public laws

Remedied: "handed over for punishment. Some editors adopt Dyce's emendation *render'd*" (Riverside, 1,522)

73 At heaviest answer.

At heaviest answer: "to pay the severest penalty" (Riverside, 1,522)

BOTH

74 'Tis most nobly spoken.

ALCIBIADES

75 Descend, and keep your words.

The Senators descend, and open the gates

Open the gates: "(Presumably, the *gates* are a door in the tiring-house façade representing the *walls* of Athens; the gallery above is *on the walls*.)" (Bevington)

Enter Soldier

SOLDIER

76 My noble general, Timon is dead;

77 Entomb'd upon the very hem o' the sea;

Hem: "i.e., edge, shore" (Bevington)

78 And on his grave-stone this insculpture, which

Insculpture: "inscription" (Riverside, 1,522)

79 With wax I brought away, whose soft impression

80 Interprets for my poor ignorance.

Interprets: "acts as an interpreter" (Charney, 146)

ALCIBIADES

81 [Reads the epitaph] "Here lies a

> **Here . . . gait**: "These lines bring together two separate epitaphs in Plutarch's account of Timon; since they are contradictory, Shakespeare would certainly have deleted or revised in a final version." (Riverside, 1,522)

82 wretched corse, of wretched soul bereft:

> **Corse**: "corpse" (Riverside, 1,522)

83 Seek not my name: a plague consume you wicked

84 caitiffs left!

> **Caitiffs**: "wretches" (Mowat, 186)

85 Here lie I, Timon; who, alive, all living men did hate:

86 Pass by and curse thy fill, but pass and stay

87 not here thy gait."

> **Gait**: "journey" (Bevington)

88 These well express in thee thy latter spirits:

> **Latter spirits**: "recent sentiments" (Bevington)

89 Though thou abhorr'dst in us our human griefs,

90 Scorn'dst our brains' flow and those our

> **Brains' flow**: "i.e. tears" (Riverside, 1,522)

91 droplets which

92 From niggard nature fall, yet rich conceit

> **Niggard**: "miserly (in comparison with the son's abundance)" (Wright, 99); **rich conceit**: "ingenious fancy" (Riverside, 1,522)

93 Taught thee to make vast Neptune weep for aye

> **Neptune**: "i.e., the sea (literally, the Roman god of the sea)"; **aye**: "ever" (Mowat, 188)

94 On thy low grave, on faults forgiven. Dead

95 Is noble Timon: of whose memory

96 Hereafter more. Bring me into your city,

97 And I will use the olive with my sword,   **Use . . . sword**: "combine
peace with war"
(Riverside, 1,522)

98 Make war breed peace, make peace stint war, make each **Stint**: "stop"
(Riverside, 1,522)

99 Prescribe to other as each other's leech.   **Leech**: "physician"
(Riverside, 1,522)

100 Let our drums strike.

Exeunt

Works Cited

Asimov, Isaac. *Asimov's Guide to Shakespeare.* Vol. 1, The Greek, Roman, and Italian Plays, New York: Avanel Books, 1970, 132-145.

Bevington, David, Ed. *The Complete Works of William Shakespeare,* Volume VI. New York: Bantam Books, 1988, unpaginated.

Charney, Maurice, Ed. *The Life of Timon of Athens.* New York: The New American Library, 1965.

Hinman, Charlton, Ed. *The Life of Timon of Athens.* Baltimore: Penguin Books, 1964.

Merriam-Webster. *Collegiate Dictionary,* 11th Ed. Springfield, Massachusetts, 2006.

Mowat, Barbara A., and Paul Werstine, Eds. *Timon of Athens.* New York: Washington Square Press, 2001.

Shakespeare, William. *The Riverside Shakespeare.* 2nd Edition. Boston: Houghton Mifflin Company, 1997, 1,489-1,525.

Williams, Stanley T., Ed. *The Life of Timon of Athens.* New Haven: Yale University Press, 1919.

Wright, Louis B., and Virginia A. LaMar, Eds. *Timon of Athens.* New York: Washington Square Press, 1967.

Printed by BoD™in Norderstedt, Germany